MW01492513

PR

BLOOD FOR SAIL

"Miles has created a very sympathetic protagonist . . . . Miles' deliberately paced, gripping narrative enables readers to really encounter this gruesome voyage of the damned. A textured, riveting portrait of a good man caught in a horrifying situation."

Kirkus Reviews

"*Blood for Sail* is a spiraling whirlpool of a story with all of the chaos, pain, and shock that come with evil schemes and the tragedy of good people confronting a nightmare scenario. It is a timely and provocative yarn about power without conscience set against those with faith. It makes you keep thinking— Could this really happen?"

Anna Grace Bentley
Chair of Missions Committee
First Presbyterian Church of West Chester, PA

"Start reading *Blood for Sail* and right away you won't want to put it down. From the beginning, the intrigue builds. Although it is a novel, *Blood for Sail* has more truth in it than a typical work of fiction. This is precisely what makes it more interesting to read. The story takes you through all kinds of feelings such as sadness, anger, and hope.

"A good study of Central and South America, the book's plot concerns a pastor's journeys among people from those places. The novel's world has theological foundations that surface through the main character's background and experiences.

(continued)

"At present, there are so many families coming to the USA in order to find a better place to live, and many of these families have encountered the same situations that are described throughout *Blood for Sail*. This book would be a great resource for a small group discussion centered on the evils of human trafficking of all kinds."

Rev. Lilian L. Cotto, United Methodist Pastor
Coordinator of Latino Ministries of the Eastern Pennsylvania
Conference

"The protagonist in *Blood for Sail* is chillingly relatable to anyone who has tried to justify personal desires by appealing to a higher power. The pastor's disturbing fall from naivete and his furtive attempts to navigate the horrifying circumstances he encounters draw the reader in. The author's descriptive prose shines a light on one man's quest against the backdrop of a continent's beauty and pain."

The Rev. Caroline Cupp, M.Div.
Executive Pastor, Bioethicist, and Hospital Chaplain
First Presbyterian Church of West Chester, PA

"A taut and gripping thriller, *Blood for Sail* carries the reader on a voyage reminiscent of Conrad's *Heart of Darkness*. Vibrant in its imagery and spellbinding in its sense of foreboding, the book swallows us into a realm that, at one and the same time is unthinkable as well as an apt metaphor for the socio-political inequities of our time. I was impressed by the depth of research into geographical, maritime, and theological issues that form the foundation of this compelling novel. I wholeheartedly recommend this book for avid readers as well as for church groups interested in discussing Latin and South American issues in a theological context."

The Rev. Dr. David W.G. Dickey, D.Min.
Pastoral Counselor and Ordained Minister of the Presbyterian Church, USA

BLOOD FOR SAIL

A NOVEL

DIANE ROSIER MILES

**DOVE IN THE
WILD WOOD**

Dove in the Wild Wood Books LLC

Dove in the Wild Wood Books LLC
112 Longfields Way
Downingtown, PA 19335

DOVE IN THE
WILD WOOD

Blood for Sail is a work of fiction. Names, characters, places, and incidents are the product of the author's imagination or are used fictitiously. Any resemblance to events, locales, or persons, living or dead, is entirely coincidental. Any mentioned brand names and trademarks remain the property of their respective owners, bear no association with the author, and are used for fictional purposes only.

Bible quotations are from the *World English Bible* in the public domain.

Edited by Sherry Mooney
Cover design and formatting by www.ebooklaunch.com
Logo design by Betty Martinez

Contact the author at dianerosiermiles@gmail.com.

First Edition

ISBN 978-0-578-39320-9

Library of Congress Control Number: 2022907265

Dedication

This novel is dedicated with a grateful heart to my husband of thirty-five years, Ed, in thanks for all of the tender and supportive ways he has stood by my side. Looking forward, I also dedicate this book to our son, Eddie, in the hope that the story inspires him to help those in need whenever he can.

BLOOD FOR SAIL

CHAPTER ONE

The call to a new life came while I stood in a wide-brim hat pondering the habits of Gladiolus Kirov. I was lost in gardener's thoughts in the sunshine. As was often the case, I was confronted by math as I guessed the number of inches between the Stella de Oro daylilies naturalized in my flowerbed. The Kirovs would nestle between them.

Older but not wiser, I'd forgotten my tape measure; then I remembered that my right foot was ten inches long. I had a little chuckle at God's provision. How kind it was of him to make my appendage a stand-in ruler. If my foot had been just a half size bigger, fractions would have made me too nervous to plant a thing. A sleek gray catbird called to me happily from the magnolia trees, but he didn't know the math, either, so there I stood, special-order bulbs in hand, calculating and counting, in a spring wind slightly perfumed.

I was advised by the small print on the Kirov packet to leave no fewer than three inches but no more than five between companion plants, or about half an old-man-foot. Still, my ancient farmer genes were helpfully guiding me in another direction. As I rubbed the corms' pointy tops with my thumb, their flaky tunics rustling under my finger, I gave up on the crowded daylily bed altogether. I had many other options. We were blessed with nearly an acre of yard, a veritable suburban kingdom, and I have to say it was a point of holy pride.

Pushing my floppy hat aside, I squinted to get a good look around my South Carolina property to estimate where I might plant my new purple-and-white, ruffled hybrid bulbs. Not under the sawtooth oaks — too shady. Not too close to the bird feeder — the interloping squirrels would dig up the bulbs. Finally, I reckoned that the gladioli would have to be planted in a due-eastern exposure against the brick backbone of the house, for abundant morning light and steady support for their statuesque stems. Like so many of us in this life, eventually the flowers would need something strong to lean on.

I mopped my brow with my linen shirtsleeve, avoiding the metal snaps on the cuff, which would've branded me with their searing heat. My eyes stung with dripping perspiration and sunscreen, and these dulled my vision for a moment. I blinked in a fluttering spasm to clear my sight. A trickle of salty sweat ran down the crease above my lip and into my mouth. I licked my lips. My beard, which I could no longer remember as chestnut brown, was wilting, greasing my collar with oily droplets that would complicate the stain removal in the laundry.

It was hot. With a sigh of resignation, temporarily defeated by Nature, I returned the bulbs to their mesh package. It would not be an act of kindness to put anything so fragile into strange dirt on such a day. The bulbs wouldn't be able to make a home of it. The weather was too sweltering. I would wait for a day with protective cloud cover, which would shield both me and the bulbs. The morning advanced. As I thought about where I might get a good price for gas for the lawn mower, I had a powerful craving for sweet tea.

At ten o'clock on this particular morning, the sun was already flinging pointed beams at Carlton Street, where I lived. It was Ash Wednesday, which jogged my landscaping memory in a way that I hoped wasn't irreverent. Later that day, I would attend church services, but at that moment I turned from planting to shoveling out the living room fireplace to fertilize my flowerbeds. I went indoors, wiping my feet on the mat as I'd been trained, and set aside the brass-trimmed, wrought-iron screen that shielded the hearth. Behind the screen, a small hill of ashes lay ready for repurposing. It was streaked with multiple shades of grey, like my beard.

I mused as I worked in the fireplace, remembering the last time that I had, myself, administered repentance ashes. It had been two years. Parishioners in a long respectful line had lowered their eyes and folded their hands as they came forward humbly to me, their pastor, to receive sacred swipes on their foreheads. Stained glass reflections from above the altar had gilded the sanctuary carpets with vermillion circles. The air was solemn with ritual. Life and death and resurrection resonated in our hearts in the ancient rite.

I had never felt my pastoral responsibilities more acutely than when I was touching human flesh. The impression of skin on skull arising through my fingertips with electric urgency made real to me exactly what was at stake. For me, on Ash Wednesday, souls took on a near-tangible, corporeal essence, and the repentance ashes reminded me that I had much work to do as a spiritual father before every person entrusted to my care inevitably dissolved into dust.

Under the circumstances, my memories are now mercurial things, coming in waves and then rolling away. I retired from the pastorate at the first indication that I could no longer remember the Lord's Prayer all the way through. At the time, I let my mental faculties tell me when it was time to go, not my fatty liver or my bank account. In deciding, I managed to separate my emotions from my intellect long enough to objectively evaluate my effectiveness as a clergyman.

For example, I realized that I was no longer attracted to scholarly research. The reference books that I used in a consulting role for the synod went unused. I discovered that I wanted only my conversational Bible to read. I wanted the straight raw Word, marked at my favorite passages with silk ribbons, in case I could no longer remember their locations with the rapidity that I'd once possessed. So, although I still wanted to read God's thoughts, I no longer aspired to formalize discussing them for a living.

Also, I lost the desire to write for the denominational magazine. Frankly, I didn't care what anybody else believed anymore. I had done my best to educate and leave a worthwhile impression in that world of influence, which was buffeted by the latest social causes and controversies. Let people work out their own salvation.

I realized I was growing crotchety. Everything was an irritant. I could barely keep my patience when an infant began to bawl during his baptism, for instance, and I was unable to find the cacophony charming, as in years past. It made my stomach hurt. The slyly observant grandma in celebratory chiffon at the font narrowed her eyes when she saw me grit my teeth at the noise. How could anyone possibly think that *her* grandson was an aggravation?

Finally, and most dangerously, I had my first impulse to murder somebody when an argument arose in a council meeting over the new color planned for the ladies' bathroom stalls. The final straw was when I stood to express my indignation, but I could not remember the name of the ignoramus who demanded that the color be pink and always pink, for that was the signature palette of true femininity. And how did what's-his-name know? I was done with trifling things and trifling people. It was time to step down. Yes, I entered a kind of private journey with the Lord, a quiet walk where I could really be myself, and a stroll that I thought might be my final walk home to his heavenly house. I retired.

But on this Ash Wednesday, I carefully brushed away the cinders heaped upon the fireplace grate, getting soot in my shaggy eyebrows, and generally making a gritty, choking mess as I traipsed back and forth to the yard with my bucket full of nourishing calcium carbonate. It was oak ash in the bucket, not Palm Sunday fronds, but nevertheless the cinders put me in a penitential mood. "Remember that you are dust," I quoted softly. "And to dust you shall return."

Such is a theologian's turn of mind. For the mature plants, I sprinkled the fireplace ashes around their roots, sifting the ash through my gloves, a handful at a time. I worked the ashes into the ground with my metal spade, sprinkling just a bit more on top of the soil where, hopefully, it would lie loose to repel the slugs. Loving the Lord's creatures as I did, I could barely bring myself to actually kill a slug, and I preferred to inconvenience them until they left, if possible. With the newer plantings, I prudently dabbed around their drip lines. The wind picked up, but luckily it didn't dislodge the ash and blow it into my nostrils, because I'd not put on a protective mask as I usually do. It reminded me too much of the sorrowful Time of COVID.

After all this fetching and digging into the earth, I looked up with satisfaction to the almost-spring sky with my spade paused, midair. I inhaled deeply and smiled. I thanked God for everything that I'd ever survived. I'm sure I appeared to be giving allegiance to some invisible being overhead. Some would have thought me a pagan supplicant to the nature idols, kneeling as I was, there in the sun. The only thing missing was a drink offering. The thought of it made my mouth water for tea again. Then, unexpectedly, there was the sound of someone rushing. I recognized the jog of my spouse getting a move on.

What could that be? I ignored a plump robin's chirp in the daffodils to listen to a curious conversation. Through the open kitchen windows, I heard my Candace trek to the ringing phone, greet a stranger excitedly, and then slam the screen door brusquely behind her to run to the flowerbed where I knelt. The small webs of capillaries on my girl's cheeks were flushed with pink excitement, and in the middle of the rosiness sat her prim nose, powdered with the white flour that she'd been using to roll out cream biscuits with her new marble pin. Candace bounced up and down in her madras tennis shoes as much as her seventy years would allow.

"It's Majestic Waves Cruises!" Candy whispered, pointing to the phone. Her eyes were glowing with happiness. "I think we made it!" She punctuated her opinion with a little comic curtsy, as if it were necessary for talking to royalty, given the "Majestic" part.

I put down the corms and tools. Could it be true? When we had retired from the church after thirty seasons, Candy and I decided to channel our unrequited wanderlust into outings on the Great Deep, the world's oceans. Perhaps that's what comes of an intense reading of Bible stories about Saint Paul's shipwrecks and his miracles done for sailors and island natives. After I retired from the clergy roster, I set about my own study of the mystical book of Acts, for my own edification, not worrying about being deemed heretical in the pulpit by a congregation accustomed to the limiting doctrines of our denomination. I became a free thinker!

I had longed to know more about the ways of the Spirit. I felt that more knowledge would be important for my personal growth as a Christian. In spending more time with Saint Paul in my retirement, and reflecting on his closeness to the Holy Spirit, I found that I got inspired and positively agitated and wanted to go to sea. Imagine! What a wild goal for an aging man, and one worried about his fading memory! But if Saint Paul could sail off into the horizon, and do so as an elderly man, why couldn't I? I was still fairly hardy and vigorous, and gardening had kept me nimble. My memory wasn't quite what it was, but I decided that no moss would ever grow on my old sinner's feet, especially if somebody else paid my fare!

Taking a chance, then, I had put myself forward as a prospective Protestant chaplain for the cruise lines. I thought that I would be able to handle the duties, which I surmised to be comparatively light. I would no longer have to convene large committees, for instance. Candace, always my supportive helpmate, could not have been more pleased to aspire to cruising. To us, the seas were almost like role models: The oceans' advancing years have not in any way weakened their vitality, and my wife and I wanted to follow suit. We could just see ourselves on the cover of *AARP Magazine*, in our sailors' hats and billowing cottons and suntans. We deserved some fun!

Also, there was the significance of the work. Souls gliding on foamy cruises still require spiritual counsel, comfort, and care. People bring their problems with them when they go on a holiday, and new issues are bound to develop, too, particularly on the longer cruises. Regrettably, married couples still quarrel. Children still disobey. Conflicting worldviews, financial challenges, and the dynamics of interpersonal dominance don't change on a vacation. The confines of shipboard life, even luxurious confines, can make existing relationship problems even worse.

And human mortality does not cease on a pleasure cruise. In fact, every year, hundreds of persons depart the ocean liner for the afterlife and expire at sea, via natural causes or through accidents or by all manner of illicit and criminal escapades. For instance, younger people traveling with known illnesses die unexpectedly. Older people thought to be in fantastic physical shape simply pass away in their sleep. Depressed people jump overboard, and drunks fall down the stairs. Then there was the woman who got too much sun, meowed like a cat, climbed the main mast, and accidentally hanged herself in the rigging!

Yes, on the high seas, both souls and waters roil in subterranean shadows, and interaction with either is risky. Pastors are needed at sea. I can understand why the Lord sends them afloat.

Hence, my wife and I believed that we might be of some small, divine use on the oceans, and that we might also be able to see the world beyond Glenville, South Carolina, our home. Unfortunately, about a thousand other retired couples had exactly the same idea, which turned our desire to minister at sea into a competition. As far as I could tell, I had no special qualifications that would make me a standout candidate. I was a dedicated, but typical, Protestant pastor. To cruise and to be of service on the oceans, there was only one way that we could afford it: for me to go as a chaplain. If the Lord wanted us to sail, he would make a way, we believed.

But prior to this sunny morning, our hopes had lapsed. After about a year without a response to our job application (for Candy and I came as a package deal or not at all), I had begun to accept that God had not called me to sail across the salty meridians in my retirement. No matter, then; I decided that I would plant flowers on my portion of terra firma and cultivate contentment. My spiraling sweet peas and overflowing clematis would serenely climb my twig tuteur, and they would bring God glory as my own landlubber's fragrant Ebenezer. I practiced acceptance.

If I were not permitted by God to sail, then I would sow, and with perennials, too. We optimists plant bulbs, for we expect to be around for quite a while to take care of them. We intend to enjoy the fruits (and flowers) of our labor. If the Lord permitted me to live a long life, albeit on land, then I would be grateful for the grace, and plant determined things, things that root in hard, to endure. I was perfectly content to do my gardening on a solid, not a liquid, field, although my harvest would be flower buds, not seafaring souls.

Or so I thought.

In a moment's time, however, the terroir of my heart quickly changed. With one phone call from Majestic Waves, a longing that I had thought superficial emerged as from a deep, coursing wellspring. I was not so nonchalant and magnanimous about where I would spend my golden years as I had believed. Below the surface of my acceptance at being rejected for the coveted chaplain's job, I still pined for the ocean. Paul's adventures at sea really had impacted me. I daydreamed about watching raspberry-hued sunsets from under a striped blanket on a deck chair, and in idle hours I could almost smell the trade winds wafting the scent of salt and cinnamon.

Also, I confess that I felt regret at never having made more money. As a pastor with a small congregation, Candy and I had never been able to put much aside. Throughout our whole marriage, we had made due with little disposable income. Perhaps a cruise chaplain's salary would supplement my pension. It would ensure that we would never know serious deprivation and provide some rewards for all of our material sacrifices over the years.

I took the phone from my wife. Looking at Candace with a lump of anxiety in my throat, I wondered if we were actually going to live on a ship. My pulse quickened. Who would mind the tulips? Anticipation made my hand shake.

"Yes, this is Pastor James Atterley. How may I help you?" One of the most important conversations of my life in that instant commenced. It went very fast, too fast. In short, the phone call was a sales pitch, and totally unnecessary, for I was most assuredly already sold. In retrospect, I could hear the recruiter's voice clearly but not God's.

Candy watched my face intently for more insight. She stood first on one foot and then on the other. She grimaced. She grinned. She clutched her fingers on top of her head as if she were making a great effort to keep her enthusiasm from steaming out through her hair follicles. Her lips formed into, "Well? Well?" as the phone call progressed.

"An offer to be a cruise ship chaplain! Hallelujah! We accept!" I wasn't coy. I didn't negotiate. That deep wellspring in my heart became a gulley washer, and in that moment, I would've signed anything. My desire was stronger than my discernment.

Candace collapsed into an Adirondack chair on the deck. She was overcome with joy. I thought that she might hyperventilate. She fanned herself with her open hand.

I repeated everything about the job offer's terms for my wife's sake. "A nine-month tour of Latin America. Is that so? Very interesting. Free passage for myself and spouse. Outstanding! Conduct daily worship services, yes. Observe religious holidays, yes. Be flexible in a multi-cultural environment, naturally. Be available for private solace in unexpected circumstances such as bereavement, of course."

The recruiter listed a few other requirements that I remembered from the original job application, such as a willingness to cooperate with the medical staff and a promise to emphasize customer service. "Well, it sounds wonderful! It's like a dream come true!" I turned to my wife, who was beaming. "I'll wait for your offer letter and start making plans to join Majestic Waves. We're so excited! Thank you, thank you again!"

"There's just one more thing," Mrs. Kimball, the recruiter, said. She cleared her throat. Her tone changed. I thought I heard her become quite deliberate with her words, as a lawyer would be, or a policeman. "You will have to sign a non-disclosure agreement. You will never talk or write about this cruise. You will not even take any photos." Mrs. Kimball then became the college professor, explaining everything to a lowly student. "Majestic Waves is bringing new services to the cruising public, and we want to be able to evaluate the results of this trip in private, with our experts, at first. We call it post-marketing surveillance."

I had to keep everything a secret? That was odd. I didn't like the sound of that. "Well, I don't know. I suppose . . . ." I looked at my lovely Candace. I didn't want to disappoint her by taking more time to consider this sterling opportunity. I was at a crossroads, and stumbling. I felt pressured but eager.

"We know it's an unusual request. You'll be compensated for complying," Mrs. Kimball said. She then became the unctuous encourager. "We've eliminated a hundred other applicants to choose you, James. Many pastors would do anything for the opportunity that we've saved for you. Come join us. Be one of us."

"How so? I mean, what do you have in mind, about compensation?" I could see that Candace was no longer even listening to the phone call and was already lounging onboard in her imagination. Her eyes looked faraway, gazing on cresting waves. She was thinking about getting a big fruity drink with a little umbrella in it. It would be painful for me to summon her back to sweet tea in a glass jar on the porch.

Mrs. Kimball continued her sales salvo. "We've planned a large bonus for you at the end of the cruise. Very substantial. In any currency you'd like, sent to any bank. We're certain you'll find it attractive. And it might be great for a person at your stage of life, after you've worked so hard. Pastors don't make nearly what they're worth, do they?"

God forgive me, I discovered that I could be bought. I had never had any money to speak of in my entire life, and I was tempted. In my mind's eye, I could see a little garden shop to own and manage in my golden years. We'd give it a snappy, catchy name. I could put a little painted patio set out front, and I could surround it with terracotta pots full of yellow nasturtiums. My friends would come and tell me what a beautiful store I owned. They'd stroke the brass doorknobs and admire the awnings. If I did well, I could play golf every Wednesday. Candace would be able to have a new stove. Maybe we could even afford to install a double wall oven, her absolute dream.

In only a few fleeting moments, my desire to learn more about the life of Saint Paul morphed into a business transaction, and one laced with bait. I decided on the spot. I swallowed my misgivings. After all, what could the cruise line possibly have to hide? Their business was sailing languorously around in circles, in the sunshine, for heaven's sake. Cruising was one of the world's most harmless pursuits. It made people happy. I could even argue that it was a healing profession, restoring one's health and vim and vigor, for everyone, even unbelievers.

I just had to make sure. I could say that I tried. "I'll only be performing a chaplain's services, correct?"

"Correct."

"I won't be handling money on the sabbath or doing endorsements?" These were the two most potentially compromising activities I could think of at the time, how quaint.

"Not at all."

I blinked and took a leap of faith. "All right, no problem. Yes, send the non-disclosure agreement along with the offer letter and I'll sign it."

"Fantastic! We'll be sending the documents out today. Welcome to Majestic Waves Cruise Lines, Pastor Atterley! We know you'll be a valuable asset. Good luck!" Evelyn Kimball's enthusiasm echoed in my ears, which were tingling with adrenaline, and instantly she hung up, before I changed my mind. I never heard her voice again.

I looked at the cell phone in my hand. My heart was rising in my chest, beating as if I'd run a mile. I realized that I'd just made an enormous commitment, with very little information, to people I barely knew, in an act of spontaneity unequal to anything I'd ever done in a long, thoughtful, well-considered life. Lord? I prayed. Oh, Lord, I said.

Slowly, I gave the phone back to Candace. She kissed it and then kissed me. Her broad smile transformed my anxiety into guilt-free exultation. Everything was all right. Candace was happy. I had made my wife proud, every husband's goal. I felt like a prize. I felt like a player.

"Ahoy, matey!" my darling said, rushing into my arms.

"Anchors aweigh!" I responded.

Then logic forced its way in. Despite my recent impulsiveness, I'm a planner. So much for the fantasy of opening my own garden shop. I sat down with my wife on the steps to the deck. "This means we should probably sell the house. It's been on our mind, remember? I don't want to rent out the place while we're away, do you? No goal of being a landlord, right? We might even find a town where we want to resettle, maybe with some ex-pats, and never return, you know?"

Candace searched my face as I spoke. I hated to be the cause of her moving so sharply from exultation to reflection, but the issue had to be faced. I'd just decided off the cuff to move us to Latin America. All of a sudden, I was aware of all the details!

"Oh, James, I think it has to be sold," Candace agreed. She reached out and held my hand, waiting to see if I had further comment. "We'll be in the best position if the house doesn't hold us back."

The sale of our home had long been a painful topic, especially as we approached retirement, because it was related to another sensitive issue: God had not given us children and we had no heirs. In the early years of our marriage, we had hoped to fill our three bedrooms with cooing babies, but, over time and with the finality of infertility, our dreams for parenthood gradually faded. Of course, while God can do anything, he never healed us of some mysterious physical abnormality. Or perhaps it was a shortcoming in my character that had made God see fit not to reproduce my predispositions in our children.

Hope is a difficult thing to extinguish, though. It has a high-octane flame. Late into our forties, my mate and I had still tried to conceive. We kept our bedrooms waiting for offspring, down to piles of snowy diapers stacked inside the closets. We bought toys. We stockpiled coloring books. We refused to give up hope. In our own master suite, Candy and I still prayed every time after our lovemaking that in our embrace, a new life had been formed.

Alas, it never was, as the splash of thick red clots on white cotton confirmed to Candace every month during her woman's time. My darling wife would sit in private, in the bathroom, and weep and weep. She felt paupered and bereft, completely inconsolable. Comforting her with gentle whispers was useless. Her shoulders stiffened at my touch.

As for me, I had no words with which to accost the bloodstains. I kept my grief inside, silent, hidden. Eventually, we used the diapers that we'd stored for babies as common dust rags instead. That was a terrible day! Our aspirations were ashes. When my wife went to the grocery, I packed up the toys and angrily drove them to Goodwill as a donation, incensed at our fate and vowing never to let Candy know how stricken I was that I could not fill her womb with a son or a daughter. Nothing but lifeless blood, only inanimate clots, came from me!

"You want to give all this stuff away?" the worker said as he unloaded my car at the drive-up. "The price tags are still on." Some little bells on a puppet jangled as he unpacked.

"Mind your own business!" I snapped in a rare moment of pique.

Then, as best we could, Candace and I transplanted our desire for children into the nurturing of our flower garden. Some childless couples choose to love dogs. We chose black-eyed Susans. It's true, we never rejoiced at the birth of a long-awaited baby as Hannah and Sarah had done in the Bible, but Candy and I had been given each other's companionship, as well as the shared delight of the flowers that emerged from the soil every season. In this way, we were fertile. We thought of ourselves as a couple of companion plants. Let God's will be done.

We shared what we'd been given with our congregation. Often on Sundays, our roses graced the altar. Our lilies filled the narthex at Easter. Our gladioli were given as gifts at baby showers held in the church basement, which my wife and I did not resent at all, though childless. Our bearded irises were shared at funerals. Our peonies were grouped in arrangements on tables at the ladies' fundraisers, and our camellia shrub clippings illuminated the dark corners of the church offices with their crimson buds at Christmastime. Our petite carnations even went to the prom in delicate corsages and boutonnieres, in a project the teens supervised that was sponsored by a local craft store. In these ways, Candace and I made our contribution to the generations.

Our memories were full of relationships that had begun and flourished because of our garden. Technically, after I retired we had no reason to preserve any property that we owned for posterity, but finally selling our home and our garden to go cruising would be an official acknowledgement that neither children nor grandchildren would ever be in our future, and that we were not only infertile but also elderly. My fear was that we would have to be cautious not to see the sale of the home and the garden as the ultimate expression of our personal failure.

I might not have worried. After the job offer came, I don't think that Candy ever pulled up the kitchen blinds again to look fondly at our backyard. The garden became a relic from a different era, something previously beloved, then forgotten. Candace disconnected from it, emotionally. To her, the telephone call from Majestic Waves was a sign of favor from above and the prompt to an unanticipated but wonderful future. The garden was no longer needed for fulfillment. "Gary down the street is a realtor. Let's give him a call," Candace said.

And I did, that very morning of Ash Wednesday. I pulled my neighbor away from his woodworking bench to announce, to his surprise, that we were decamping.

"Gary, my friend, we've decided to pull up stakes and hit the waters. We need you to sell our home. I took a job as a cruise ship chaplain."

"You're doing what? You're going where?" Gary asked. "I thought I'd see them carry you out one day," he observed, rather insensitively, too, I might add.

A few weeks later, in late March, not only were my wife and I "home-less," but also "furniture-less" and "yard-less." Luckily, during our realtor's open houses, the flowers on our property had looked their floral best, for it was springtime. The glowing forsythia bushes that lined our stone walkway pulsed like a neon arrow pointing to Eden, and the foliage almost singlehandedly sold the house. Candy complained that for his fee, Gary didn't have to do much but unlock the front door to let people inside. The property spoke for itself. Kindred gardener spirits were thrilled with our designs, and the fact that the flowers, shrubs, trees, and vines had been loved like children showed through.

Finalizing the sale of our home proved easy. In the real estate contracts, we set the date for the home's transfer to its new owners, Drs. Jason and Jill Carmichael, both dentists, and fantasized more and more about the *Grand Rapina*, our new cruising "house-boat." I liked the Carmichaels very much, but I couldn't escape a vision that I had of them applying compost to the echinacea and then sticking their fingers in my mouth, and that limited the prospects for friendship right from the start, I'm afraid. Jason and Jill had two little boys, and I'm sure they enjoyed building a treehouse. I hope they didn't stomp on the hostas.

As we cleared our home, folding, tossing, and packing, we had a crying jag when Candace put out on the curb the bassinet that we'd kept in our attic for so long. Years ago, I'd flung a bedsheet over it to hide it. At the time, it was next to impossible to dispose of the bassinet without Candy seeing, so, like my grief, I covered it up.

When my wife yanked off the fabric, wondering what it was concealing, she gasped. Tears streamed down her face. "Oh, our cradle, our cradle," she moaned. Candace rolled it to the street as carefully as if it contained a live infant. She dropped it off and then went back to embrace it one last time. She was sobbing so that I thought the neighbors might hear her. I couldn't help myself. I joined in. Our weeping spell was like a river of purged disappointments. We clung to one another. Then, blessedly, the pain was gone, like a wound that had been opened with a sharp scalpel and cleaned and stitched. We were absolutely, deeply, ready to move on.

At the last moment, as with any conscience-stricken father, I almost felt that I was abandoning innocent dependents by moving away. After all, I had seen these plants "grow up.". I left explicit written instructions for the new owners on how this plant liked to be fertilized, and how that one liked to be pruned. Secretly, I harvested seeds from my favorites, in case I should ever own a garden again, and kept them in a satin pouch in my Bible. Looking back, I take that reticence as an ominous sign. If only I had known.

We probably could have stayed with friends for free, but Candace and I relocated into a nearby motel for a few days before we joined the *Grand Rapina*, enjoying the quaint waffle house that was attached to the motel. I think now that I, too, was severing emotional connections and anything that might have held me back from committing to our new future, so I didn't want to rely on people I'd once been close to. It's funny how human beings protect their vulnerability.

At the motel, we woke up every morning smelling blueberry syrup through the walls. After our daily breakfasts of pancakes and sausage, my spouse and I sat out on the restaurant's patio, playfully affecting the identity of those who are well-traveled by ocean liner. We were evolving. We tried on our emerging roles as cruise ship passengers. It never occurred to us that we might not succeed. We aimed to become cosmopolitan voyagers.

For example, we developed an intense interest in checking the weather, as if all of our lives we had had reason to monitor the tempestuous paths of hurricanes, squalls, and tsunamis. We became suitably outraged by the very idea of port taxes. We spent one quite pleasant afternoon pondering the advantages of dual citizenship. We decided to study a foreign language to be well-equipped for life abroad, but we could never select just one, for suddenly all of the languages under

Babel seemed so very relevant and so naturally interesting. At last, Candace and I determined that it would be better to be conversational in at least half a dozen tongues, since we were going to see the whole world, which was rather more than what had been promised by Majestic Waves in a nine-month contract to Latin America, but we were ambitious and excited by our new prospects.

I must admit right now, we became blinded by our enthusiasm.

We had a dream with a moral motivation, and a way to finance it appeared. Doors opened. Obstacles vanished. Surely, the opportunity to become a cruise line chaplain was from the Lord, we thought. Anyone would have believed so.

If Candace and I had sought more guidance from God, perhaps I would not be compelled to give this statement about an international maritime catastrophe. I have been sworn to tell the truth to the authorities. Officials in high places assigned with dispensing justice demand to know what happened onboard the luxurious *Grand Rapina*, and why it occurred, and why I survived it. The world looks to me to give answers.

I am at a loss to tell them. The authorities seem to think that because I am a pastor, I have insights and explanations. I am not ashamed to say that I, myself, am traumatized. What God permits confuses me. I can't explain the depravity of human nature that began with the Fall in the Garden. No evil of this kind was ever found among my flowers. Every day, I looked out on my garden and, like God, I said that it was good, only good.

How could a seventy-two-year-old-man, an educated, spiritual person, have been so wrong about a call from the Lord? God permitted me to descend into danger and terror, more than just my own, on the *Grand Rapina*. Why? I was not Noah, but like him I found myself in a turbulent, sea-tossed ark, trying to save people. A storm of medical horror came, for which I was unprepared. Would God have removed me from this misadventure if I had consulted him more earnestly before I rashly gave up my South Carolina home? Or was I, even with the weight of my doubts and uncertainties about to drown me, in the right place, fulfilling God's will to help my brothers and sisters of color?

I'm not sure. On this side of heaven, I might never know.

For me, God did not walk on the waters and say, "Get out of the boat, and come."

There was no rescue. He made me stay on the ship, with the others, unsafe in the storm.

Saint Paul, can you tell me why peace did not descend on me like a dove?

Perhaps I do not know the Lord's voice at all.

But I can use mine to tell you what happened.

CHAPTER TWO

I immersed myself in studying Latin American culture, the history, the music, the cuisine, everything. I thought that a well-informed outlook would make me a better cruise ship chaplain during our route through Central and South America. While I didn't plan to compete with the tour guides I was bound to meet, a basic introduction to the Latin American way of life would at least make me a knowledgeable travelling companion for people I'd be ministering to, as well as a good conversationalist with Candace.

Once we'd made our decision to ride with the *Grand Rapina*, I looked for resources to educate myself about this part of the world that I'd never experienced. I found that my curiosity was invigorated by research as in the early days of my career. The subject matter that I found so exotic held my attention rapt, and my memory cooperated with renewed capacity. I absorbed details and data easily, with a fluency that heartened me, and in an ironic way my new mental dexterity affirmed that I had been right to retire. Had I become emotionally overwhelmed in full-time ministry, or bored even, and not intellectually faded, as I'd feared? Was I simply burned out by the grinding interpersonal demands and administrative duties? After all, I'd borne them for thirty years. My best qualities had been drained down to the quick, but I was elated that they appeared to be renewable resources.

I started my Latin American studies on a small scale, not wanting to get in too deep right away. The first thing that I did was to review our itinerary and ports of call, and then I turned to researching the political histories of each country, their imports and exports, demographics, and geography. I thought this was a professional and scholarly beginning, and it built on my present state of knowledge. For example, I was aware that the nations I'd be going through had their own indigenous religions that were influenced by beliefs brought by African slaves. This admixture was impacted greatly by Catholicism spread by colonial priests, with Catholicism remaining the predominant faith today, including its relatively new ideas of liberation theology born of the region's political struggles. In some Latin American countries, though, there is currently a charismatic Pentecostal awakening as well, which has been met with mixed reactions by the traditionalists in Rome. Thus, in the minds and daily practical lives of many Latin American citizens, these spiritual co-minglings often result in a soup of beliefs that some of my colleagues in the Protestant Church find distressing and unorthodox, and others, inclusive and empowering.

Interestingly, it never occurred to me that my white skin might preclude me from ever gaining anything other than a superficial understanding of Latin American culture. In the final analysis, we can only be who we are. It never occurred to me that I would never really be able to taste guava with the nuance of a native Chilean tongue, or that I would never be able to sleep with authentic Costa Rican serenity through an afternoon siesta. I did not believe that I could not walk (or sail) into Latin America and experience its essence as one born to the place.

Granted, my Caucasian skin would always partially hold me back, influencing my interpretation of Latin America, and bring South Carolina and the Lowcountry to the experience, but I never thought that my own personhood would be a total barrier to learning more about and appreciating my fellow men and women. If I had felt so limited at the outset by my race, I would have stayed home. Can any study of humankind truly be separated from the color of those who conduct it? I know now that in some ways I was extremely naïve, but I relied on my goodwill to lead the way as I entered into more awareness of Latin America.

For a bit of fun, the explorer in me began to collect postcards. These cards are still in production, despite the predominance of the paperless digital varieties, and many people find the hardcopy cards delightfully retro and chic. I'm one of them. I was so eager to see the countries of Latin America that I could not wait to physically walk on them. No, I had to hold their paper facsimiles in my hands. Via the cards that I downloaded in our hotel's internet cafe, I fetched the countries' landmarks immediately for my eyes, if not yet for my feet. A professional woman sitting next to me in the lounge with a foaming latte proved an able technical tutor as Google fed me one Latin American image after another.

"Can you speak Spanish?" the helpful woman asked between sips of her coffee. With a clatter, she rolled her chair closer to mine. Maybe she just wanted me to stop monopolizing the printer.

"Afraid not. No Spanish here, not yet."

"Let's translate these pages for you. Here. Click the translate button."

Babel had surely been conquered. I was a whiz in no time.

"We can put these on your phone, if you want."

The woman was struck by my quaint desire for paper. "You won't believe it, but I want to feel them with my hands," I said. I instantly regretted saying what might have sounded like erotic overtures. Pastors have to be careful of those impressions.

Unoffended, the nice lady smiled at me with a look of gentle toleration. I guessed that she looked at me and saw her grandfather. More images rolled out of the printer.

"Allow me to buy you another cup of coffee as thanks," I offered. "You've given of your time. I'm a better modern techie because of you."

"That's all right, the world needs free kindness now, just pass it on," the woman said. She gathered my printouts for me. As she rose to leave the lounge, I saw that her briefcase was tastefully monogrammed in gold letters. There was a time when I would have wanted their gilding on my own leather satchel. That era had passed, but I was so thankful to have made this woman's acquaintance.

Surfing online, I continued to examine colorful postcards and selected a dozen more to print out on heavy stock. In my imagination, soon I, too, would wander along the scenic beaches in Brazil, casually strolling in flip flops about the size of the native bikinis. In Mexico, I saw myself performing with mariachi musicians as they serenaded excitable restaurant patrons and passed their sombreros for tips. In Cuba, I held on for dear life in a 1950's classic car as it sped through Spanish town squares whose colonial architecture has withstood earthquakes, Captain Henry Morgan's buccaneers, smallpox, and Marxist plots.

Via the postcards, in Peru, I was able to see Mayan new moons rise eerily over the mountains and lush Inca terraces descend. In Argentina,

I could hear the petulant tango dancers stomp their passionate, insistent seductions. In my hands, on postcards that I chose from an ordinary vinyl chair in a mid-priced hotel in the States, faraway Latin America opened up to me in a steamy panorama, with brightly billed parrots flying skyward; prickly cacti stretching outward; and warm, hefty coconuts oozing their sticky milk. Soon, I would no longer be an armchair explorer, but the real thing. I couldn't wait!

Since I rarely undertake any project in a superficial way, it was not long before I learned more about the route for our cruise. My new knowledge tempered my enthusiasm for the trip, however, for I discovered the extent to which the African slave trade had formed the shameful foundation on which so many contemporary Latin American economies are based. I was ignorant of how the coffee that I enjoy in the morning is often farmed by impoverished laborers even today, with workers and their children typically living in slave-like conditions, sharing their drinking water with jungle bats from open tanks. Injustices abound and continue, generation after generation. Coffee growing in Latin America now pays so little that some workers turn to clandestinely farming poppies on their own small plots for the drug cartels to supplement their income enough to feed their families. Economic desperation is rife.

I also learned that the outbreak of coffee leaf rust is decimating modern farms with a blight that's considered incurable, even though scientists continue to try to strengthen the coffee plants through hybridization. Coffee growers and their workers have an uncertain future because of the fungal disease, and also because of the new patterns of flood and drought thought to be caused by climate change.

Some gourmet coffee-producing nations in Latin America are considering changing over to crops of tea in order to survive. And as the world's climate becomes increasingly hotter, there is even talk of coffee being grown on a commercial scale in California and Florida. In the past, only Hawaii in the States was hot enough to grow coffee beans, but now, these two additional states might serve as competition for traditional growers in Latin America.

But most of all, I learned that with only a very few exceptions, most of the governments in Latin America are so corrupt, fragile, and unpredictable that their citizens cannot count on even the most basic of services, such as clean, potable water and garbage pickup, much less fair elections and medical care. Gang violence is so predominant that governments do little about it, often because they're too weak and politically disorganized to fight it. When they lose their will to resist gang violence, the governments have even been known to participate in it. The average citizens have come to expect little from their leaders and try to survive one day at a time.

My feelings of patriotism for my own country rose uneasily within me. In my mind's eye, I saw amber waves of grain, from sea to shining sea, but also imperfect courts where corrupt judges decide the fates of hapless citizens. I wanted to see a shining city on a hill, and I did, but its brightness was dangerously clouded over. My prayer and hope was that Americans safeguard our own way of life.

As Alexander Pope bemoaned, a little learning is a dangerous thing. For starters, it begins to open your eyes, but leaves you partly blind. Hence, I became saddened that my postcards reflected the best attributes of Latin America and concealed the worst. They were a kind of idealization, even caricatures, heavily commercialized. Were the cards the result of an honest impulse to present oneself and one's culture in a positive light, or a con intended to entrap unsuspecting travelers? And what is to be blamed for such a deceit? Human nature? Tourism executives?

The dismay that I felt condensed into a small, philosophical vial. I wondered if the tourists about to cruise on the *Grand Rapina*, with all of its exclusivity and glamour and comfort, had any idea of the forces at work in troubled Latin America. Surely, my fellow travelers could not know the grim facts, and they were, like me, naïve. Reasonable, enlightened people would not knowingly choose to blithely sail on pleasure cruises through a region simmering with inequality, violence, and suppression, would they? Would they? And when God looks down from heaven, can he even tell the difference between Tijuana and the south side of Chicago?

My emotional discomfort deepened. I had mixed feelings. I began to have doubts about the whole tourism industry, and especially about the form known as cruising, with its emphasis on luxury for an elite few. What was my responsibility? Could I justify cruising by arguing that it supports financially endangered countries economically? And hadn't I been hired to perform honorable Christian services, not simply sunbathe?

I wavered back and forth. It occurred to me that all cruises probably highlight the best and hide the worst of the lands that they tour, and it might not be possible for tourists to go anywhere if I insisted that everywhere be perfect before someone go to see it. It's a broken world, so should we all just never go on vacation? Wouldn't it be possible for me to be good to people as I traveled? I thought long and hard about these paradoxes.

Despite all of the questions, in our final night in Glenville, I was excited. Moving aside the soggy paper plates, plastic cups, and chicken salad wrappers from our dinner, I spread out the postcards on our temporary table, which was the double bed in our hotel. The paisley, mass-produced bedspread was spacious, deliriously red and white in the spirit of hotel fabrics, and perfectly suited to impromptu picnics without ants. I wanted to share the postcards with my wife, who stopped eating her sliced apple dessert when she saw them.

"Where did you get those?" Candace asked as I laid out my treasure. "We haven't left South Carolina yet." She patted the bedspread with the sticky palm of her hand to try to locate the tiny salt packet that had come with her fruit. She eventually found it, camouflaged in a paisley swirl. "Would you like a bite?"

"No, it's turning brown. Look, I printed these out downstairs, in the internet lounge."

Candy put on her glasses. "You missed your calling as a photo editor. Lift that one up and let me see it," my wife said, leaning close, poking a bullfighter in Mexico City and leaving a wet fingerprint on his cape. "He's got sequins on his suit!"

I reshuffled the postcards. "Look at this one. I confess I thought Fidel Castro sitting on a fishing boat was Ernest Hemingway. Don't tell anybody. It must be the beards."

My wife dusted the salt from her hands with a quick swipe. She lowered her voice to a melodramatic, conspiratorial whisper. "Your secret is safe with me. This is the least of what I know." Candy gave each remaining card a close look with her bifocals, pausing disapprovingly at the one with the scant bikinis. "Sunscreen saves lives" was all she said under her breath, which made me nearly choke with laughter. Candace gathered the cards and piled them neatly on a night stand. "Let's go to sleep," my wife advised, yawning. "No more travelogues. Tear yourself away. It's a big day tomorrow."

My spouse slipped off her wire glasses, rubbed the bridge of her nose, and lay her head cozily against my chest on that decadent pillow-top mattress. Instantly, I heard the sound of her gentle snores, more like purrs. This was our favorite position for cuddling. Over the years, looking down on her in her slumber, I had seen the part in Candy's hair slowly grow whiter and whiter with age. It was certainly a bittersweet calendar, her fading coif.

This night, I amused myself by browsing a pocket dictionary of nautical terms. As quietly as I could so as not to wake up my love, I flipped through the pages, holding the book above her head. Shortly, I, too, was drowsy, and soon I was steeped in technicolor scenes of towering stone fortresses perched on craggy cliffs to guard strategic Caribbean harbors. In these dreams, I saw bloodthirsty pirates orgiastically counting doubloons, and Elizabethan gentlemen in frilled velvets stoically walking the plank. I heard cannons fire and the wounded shriek, too, but I was so tired from taking a melatonin pill, I didn't wake up.

In the morning, Candy and I arose at dawn. In the half light in the unfamiliar room, I accidentally stepped on my wife's toe while I searched for the coffee cups, but she forgave me once it stopped throbbing. We gathered the usual provisions common to modern tourists, and our Samsonite luggage rattled with umbrellas, walking shoes, insect repellant, lip balm, sunglasses, and binoculars. We also carried modest swimwear, dressy clothes for dinner on the *Grand Rapina*, plenty of casual tee shirts and shorts, and a chapel veil for covering Candy's head, in order to respectfully visit ancient Catholic cathedrals. Of course, I packed my clerical collars. I wore one this day, too. And I am never without a pocket Bible, New Revised Standard Version.

As we readied for our drive to the Port of Charleston, we secured in a fanny pack our cruise ship papers, passports (and two photocopies), drivers' licenses, prescription medications (including a list of our allergic reactions), credit cards, eyeglasses, cell phones, and a back-up charger. Candy persuaded me to leave off carrying a calculator, since our smart phones would do the ciphering, but I insisted on keeping my over-the-counter, anti-diarrheal pills nearby in my wallet. I have my priorities. Montezuma's Revenge necessitated careful measures.

About seven o'clock in the morning, back downstairs in the lounge, I printed out a map of Union Pier's Gate 2, and circled the location of the indoor parking lot in yellow highlighter. The cruise line had agreed to pay for all of my travel expenses, but I still had to physically store my vehicle somewhere for the length of our trip. I was vaguely uneasy about this part. I did not want to come home to hail damage or seagull droppings on my Mazda, so the indoor garage was the obvious choice.

"Do you think we should've sold the car, too?" I asked Candy. "We could've gotten a rental and saved all this parking trouble. I hope the thing starts when we get back. I thought about everything else but the car."

"Too late now. Something to think about for our next excursion."

We left the hotel and set out. The drive from Glenville to the Port of Charleston took about three hours, and all along the route we eagerly followed the cruise ship icons posted on highway signs. I ate a mango-and-almond granola bar while I drove, which Candy peeled open for me, so that I could watch the exits diligently and keep my hands on the steering wheel. For herself, Candy had brought pineapple yogurt. Already, we were thinking tropical.

When we drove into the historic district in Charleston on our way to the cruise ship terminal, the town was wide awake on a clear, glowing morning, with tourists and vendors and locals and barking dogs and scampering children churning together in the crowded City Market. The sweetgrass basket weavers, jewelry makers, shrimp boilers, and horse-and-carriage drivers were out in force. Street entertainers thumped their Gullah drums and clapped their hands. I feared that commerce might be rained out by a thunderstorm forecast for the afternoon, but I suspected that the merchants had surely dealt with the exigencies of stormy weather before, brought to them regularly by whipping hurricanes that ravaged the stately palm trees and flooded the city parks. It would be interesting to see the citizens' contingency plans. Would large tents appear? Would everyone rush for shelter in the Market Hall and Sheds?

I drove into the appropriate parking garage, where the spring sunshine immediately faded as if a curtain had been drawn. With my eyes adjusting to the gray hue of the shadow, I greeted the indoor attendant perched on a stool inside her little glass cage. Candy watched benignly as identification changed hands. My wife leaned forward and gave the slow-drawling attendant a wave of acknowledgement.

"Where ya'll headed?" the worker asked while stapling our papers. A pierce-and-crunch sound rattled on every sheet, which set my teeth on edge. Stapling sounds had never bothered me before, but this time, when they combined with the woman's unhurried way of working, I was aggravated. You would've thought we were going to the moon, with so much paperwork.

"We're going to Latin America."

The woman nodded, thinking, not sure if she were impressed. "I hear they got giant swimming pools on them ships," the attendant said. "Why folks need a pool when they is floating on the whole entire ocean of water is beyond me. If I start saving now, maybe when I'm old like you, I can afford to go. I hear the food's real good."

Candace pushed her shoulders back at being called old.

I placed the parking permit on the dashboard, and tucked my color-coded claim ticket inside my fanny pack. "Ya'll have a good trip now," the attendant drawled. "See you in nine months, I reckon." The woman slammed her little window in my face and returned intently to her crossword puzzle. She wiped the ink from her fingers onto her sweatshirt.

My employment packet from Majestic Waves had noted that a shuttle bus would take us directly to the cruise ship. After we'd parked our car, this shuttle arrived quickly. When we saw the plump van, its air conditioning and Mercedes motor were humming hospitably. The driver, a young college student on a spring break, guided us into the shuttle. He lifted our half-dozen pieces of luggage with ease. What a blessing that was! The young man was suntanned and freckled, and judging by his shaggy, white-blonde mane, he was going straight back to a pool party after he finished shuttling tourists.

"You guys feel good?" he asked, solicitous, making sure we were comfortable once inside the van. "Been waiting long?" The student hopped behind the shuttle's steering wheel. He glanced at us in his rearview mirror, leaned back, and propped his sandaled feet on the gas pedal. "I could use a cold one! My friends and me always keep a cooler of cold ones down on the beach." The young man sighed, wistful and unquenched.

"We're on our first cruise," I said, making conversation. "We're going through Latin America. I'm the new chaplain for the *Grand Rapina*."

The student replied, "That's why you got the thing around your neck, got it, right." He stifled a yawn. "I never been down that way. Too hot. Now we wait."

Candace and I looked at each other, wondering. In no rush, the young driver checked the time on his phone, responded to a text, and then gazed contemplatively at the yellow lines that separated each parking space. The indoor lot was virtually vacant. Where was everybody? A tuft of the student's blonde bangs quivered in the refreshingly air-conditioned breeze that circulated through the bus. The driver remembered his shopping list for the party. He dictated quick reminders to himself. "Stock us up on crab legs," he said into his phone, "and nachos. Mikey said get twenty pounds of ice."

I was confused by not going right to the cruise ship. "Is there something else?" I ventured. "Why the wait?"

"It's just the schedule. I have to follow the schedule."

Five minutes passed. Ten minutes passed. No other passengers jumped from the recesses of the parking lot to climb into the shuttle with us. I grew impatient.

"Well, I guess you do want nautical people to be precise," Candace joked wanly. "We can't get ahead of ourselves."

"Hmm."

Just then, a ramshackle hatchback unexpectedly rounded the garage entrance, and its smoking tailpipe led me to believe that it had barely made it. A youngish woman carrying a solitary suitcase climbed out of the car. She looked to be in her early thirties, an aspiring professional of some kind, judging from the Massachusetts college decal on her rear window. This woman had come a long way to take a cruise, if she were from Boston, a city renowned for its own port. Why had she driven all the way down South? Did the waves off of Nantucket no longer billow?

I saw the young lady head for our shuttle, walking as if on a mission, and in kitten heels. She was going to be our traveling companion, it seemed. Watching her, I remembered so well my own years of just starting out. A new car would've been an exorbitant expense for me, too, back then, considering all of my school loans. All these years later, I still can't look at a jar of peanut butter or a pack of baloney. I could understand the paradox of how the woman could seem well-educated, professional-looking, and full of a promising future, and yet still be unable to afford even a decent, presentable car. She must have come to Charleston for an important reason. Was she a manager for the cruise line? A new hire like me?

The young woman dourly approached our bus. I thought the better of my cheerful welcome. "Jenny Elihu," she said to the driver, seeking permission to approach. Climbing the shuttle steps in her low heels, the woman barely looked up from the perfunctory announcement of her name, and instead concentrated on finding a seat in the extreme back of the vehicle. She did not have a tourist's excitement, only an air of petulance.

"We're Pastor James and Candace Atterley," my wife suddenly offered, especially friendly at the idea of a new female companion, I suppose. "You can call me Candy. Have you ever been through Latin America on a cruise before? I hope I brought the right clothes." I was touched by my wife's talkative gesture of comradery. This was rare for her. She can be reticent with new people, but the trip was making her more spontaneous.

Jenny, however, was not open to making a friend. She looked at us, at me especially, with undisguised disdain. I might have been a telephone pole blocking her view of the ocean, or somebody who dripped his ice cream cone onto her beach towel. "So you're the pastor for the trip," Jenny observed tersely. "I see. I thought you would be younger." She tossed her black hair over her shoulder with an arrogant flip, settled into a seat as far away from us as possible, and pulled her dark sunglasses on. Candy and I were erased from Jenny's awareness as she resolved to look out the window and not at us.

I glanced at my wife to see if she would respond. She seemed genuinely perplexed, but she said nothing about the rudeness. Knowing Candy well, though, I could detect a little bit of pain around the corners of her gracious smile, which was not the reaction that I had expected. It seemed that Candy had for a moment really enjoyed the idea of having another female along, even though they were a generation apart in age.

Our shuttle driver all at once became seized with animation and shoved the bus into gear. It roared awake and trembled on its axles. "Here we go!" he called. "Next stop, the *Grand Rapina*!" We pulled out of the darkened garage and back into the glaring sunlight.

I took Candy's hand and squeezed it.

The first sight of the gleaming white vessel in dock, floating in all of its gargantuan splendor and surrounded by focused longshoremen moving cargo into the hull, made me gape admiringly in appreciation. So large was the ship that it was difficult to conceive of it as a work of man and not a natural wonder of Nature. I had never been so close to a cruise liner before, and for me, they'd been only the stuff of movies. I was over-awed as I looked upward to watch the ship's flag of state, registered to Panama, unfurling with crisp snaps in the azure sky. Decks upon decks, the lowest dotted with stout orange lifeboats, rose in an orderly procession above my head and into the clouds, where seagulls whirled and cried out as they flew. "It's Leviathan," I whispered, "a marvel, an ark!"

"Wow, it's unbelievable! Would you look at that!" Candace effused.

I felt a tap on my arm. Someone broke the trance that held my gaze. "Do you folks need to check in? The security line is this way," a port official pointed. I saw a cruise ship representative in the distance, behind a counter, next to an x-ray scanner. As I turned to call to my wife, I was relieved that she'd remembered to tip the shuttle driver for unloading our luggage. Finishing up, she joined me in line with our bags, helpfully collected by a porter. In a few minutes, Candy and I were inspected, photographed, and equipped with the all-important electronic boarding pass. It would be both our stateroom key and our ship's credit card.

Jenny Elihu walked right by us without speaking. Her steps were brisk. For some reason, she had special boarding privileges. No waiting in line for her. She was in quite a hurry.

"That's an interesting woman," Candy observed. "Single-minded."

"Or ill-mannered," I said.

The cruise representative gushed hospitality. "We've planned a great cruise for you! The gangway is straight ahead. Have a lovely voyage!" She slipped a map of the *Grand Rapina* into our welcome folder and presented it to us like an award. "You'll never forget this trip!"

I expected to join a serpentine line of fellow travelers at the gangway, but only two dozen or so other sojourners were preparing to board the

Grand Rapina. This dearth of guests reminded me of the mostly vacant garage. Where was everybody? Those who were in line seemed to be technical staff, given that they spoke their own language with its particular vocabulary. I heard snatches of their jargon and inside jokes, but I was surprised by their reticence to speak to me. Maybe I wasn't geeky enough? I had no canvas backpack or earbuds. Maybe it was the old timer's handshake that I offered?

No matter. I took Candy's arm affectionately. She was stiff. "A little bit nervous?" I whispered. "We're going to have a wonderful time."

"It's a new thing. We're trying new things."

Up and over the narrow gangway we went. Looking over the railings as we walked, I could see undulating, green seawater lapping to the right of the ramp and to the left. I inhaled deeply, aware that with only a few more steps, I was moving literally off of South Carolina — solid old ground that it is — and onto the inscrutable, looming Atlantic. I felt that I was leaving a refuge, my previous life, and entering into another world, one where not only the support under my feet behaved differently but also society. I would be dependent on the skill and good intentions of strangers. If something went wrong, I would not be able to drive this cruise ship back to Charleston or get out and walk home to Glenville. I was placing myself in unknown hands and going far away from the people and places that constituted my history. It's odd that the *Grand Rapina* immediately evoked a feeling of vulnerability in me. Looking back, my instincts were giving me a warning.

We walked through the ship. We caught our breath in wonder. Candace and I were instantly captivated by the vessel's sumptuous splendor. We looked up with astonishment into a soaring, ten-story atrium, filled from top to bottom with treasures. Two magnificent wrought-iron staircases swooped upward into the ether as if weightless, each staircase crowned at the top with a multi-tiered crystal chandelier sparkling like a diadem. Gold-leafed balconies were stacked one above the other to form galleries. The domed ceiling contained enormous skylights that revealed authentic sunshine and roaming clouds by day, and, as we would soon learn, artificial moonbeams and starlight by night. The gardener in me recognized fuchsia roses fresh from Columbia and creamy Holy Ghost orchids from Venezuela. These flowers filled sculptural vases that lined seemingly acres of delicately veined Italian marble floors.

Then there was the incredible fountain, located in the center of everything. It contained a buxom, larger-than-life-size mermaid. With her enticing smile of invitation, I would have expected to see such an object at a casino or a strip club, but my frame of reference for carnality was limited. The mermaid struck me as carved with exaggerated strokes, with no subtlety to her at all, but apparently the ship's designer considered her to be in good taste. Her fish-scale hips were ample and her wanton-woman nipples were wide. I would never be able to stand in front of the outlandish, immoral creature to take a photo to send home to the synod, not with a PG rating on it.

"Coralia" was the mermaid's name, according to a little plaque on the fountain. She reflected the stories of the sirens who lured sailors to die on rocky coasts. In the atrium, this monument to seduction effervesced with misty plumes that were illuminated by orange and violet laser beams, whose source was hidden cleverly. Each exuberant spout danced in rhythm to classical Latin American music. Because of my recent research, I thought that I could identify Antonio Lauro's guitar piped in from all directions. I was glad that I'd studied a bit about his music, but I wondered how he would feel about having it swirling through the voluptuous breasts of a mythical, murderous hussy.

The whole atrium space radiated lavish indulgence. We took it all in. Sofas upholstered in shining brocades and filled with plump, downy cushions were numerous. Intensely patterned chairs in bright colors were paired with plush ottomans and ready for a passenger's spontaneous resting. Velvet drapes with twirling fringes were voluminously piled on windows, the fabric's abundant folds artfully stretched across mullioned panes. Gleaming walnut and cherry side tables were plentiful. Beveled pier mirrors stood nearly ten feet high and four feet wide, I guessed. Landscapes of dappled fawns, curvaceous wood nymphs reclining on grasses, and speckled, regal birds with florid feathers and noble heads hung regally in vivid murals. I felt a theatrical, Baroque impact as I looked. To tell you the truth, I felt as if I'd wandered into a forbidden royal boudoir.

"It sort of makes you want to say, 'Off with his head!'" Candace commented dryly.

After my wife and I had feasted with our eyes, our palates were impressed. Frothing coupes of pink champagne were served by beauty-queen crew members wearing frilly, black-and-white cocktail dresses. These waitresses bowed to us, which made my wife blush at their abject subservience. "Oh, no," Candace self-consciously corrected. "No bowing, absolutely no bowing, please." I noticed that my wife did not refuse the offer of shrimp puff hors d'oeuvres, however. Knowing her, she asked for the recipe.

I took up a glass of champagne and glanced around the bon voyage party, wondering whose millionaire dream I'd fallen into. The few other guests whom I saw were not nearly as stunned as myself at the exemplary service and bawdy mermaid, and they eagerly took photos of the naked vixen, milling around to figure out where the lasers that colored her were coming from. They even set their dripping drinks down on the furniture, without thinking twice about it. At home, for such an infraction, Candace would have taken off my hand.

A handsome senior staffer, whose three-bar epaulettes indicated significant rank, approached me during the gathering. I was feeling rather good. On my last gulp of champagne, I turned to face him. Like everyone else on this ship, the man seemed to be very young. He knew all about me, but I had no idea who he was, except for the name tag on his dashing uniform that read "Vera." It was a name that I would come to hate.

"Welcome to the *Grand Rapina*, bound for the islands of the hot blooded," the officer said in a Spanish accent. The man smiled, baring his small, white teeth. "We have come ashore for provisions and essential personnel such as you, Reverend James Atterley." The man referred to my clerical collar by pointing his finger. "It took us a long time to choose you, Reverend. We trust you will keep us in God's good graces, in spite of rough sailing."

It wasn't the introduction that I'd expected. I admit I was flustered. "I'll do my best."

"And for you, it's a pity you have no chance to tell anyone about your adventure. Remember, you agreed not to tell!" The officer laughed coarsely, patted me on the back with condescending familiarity, and strode away, brushing aside the lovely servers who attended us.

Candace and I were taken aback. We watched the officer disappear into a corridor. "How inappropriate, to just walk up and say such a thing," my wife complained. "Can you explain any of that?"

Why were God's good graces going to be difficult to keep? I wondered. And why the reference to my non-disclosure agreement? An icy chill spread through me like a winter nor'easter. I'm a private person. I keep my personal life to myself. Inexplicably, on the *Grand Rapina*, the details about me already seemed to be common knowledge. In the back of my neck, where I feel stress, I felt a spasm of regret at leaving South Carolina. I acquiesced to an impulse to look back once more at the dock, which clung to the sod of my birth. Frankly, I needed reassurance. I found myself surrounded by evil mermaids and servile potion bearers and impudent officers with inside knowledge about my life. I felt as if I'd been drugged. I was vaguely faint. What was in that champagne?

"James, what are you doing?"

"Just give me a moment," I asked Candace. I placed my foaming aperitif back on a silver tray, walked away a few steps, and poked my head out of the top of the gangway. South Carolina already seemed a distant land. I wondered if I were doing the right thing, taking this chaplain's job. I wondered why my instincts were suddenly so on edge. Was the Spirit speaking to me?

In the midst of my own melancholy, I looked out on a vignette of anguish. A brown-skinned, elderly man in mismatched shoes was struggling to drag an unwieldy, lumpy sack out of a side door in the ship. It must have been the crew's entrance. The man was short and hunched, and in his tremulous grip the bag rolled this way and that. The old man leaned forward to gather his bundle, looked over his shoulder furtively, and pulled again and again with frantic effort, straining. He made me think that he was hurrying to exit the *Grand Rapina* with whatever he could scrounge. What was in the sack? Food? I'm not sure why my first thought was that the man was hungry. Of course, he dared not try to leave the cruise ship through the main atrium, but by all appearances he was sneaking out through a ship's crevice as best he could, making a break for it.

When he noticed me leaning out of the doorway above, staring down at him, the elderly man froze. He instantly dropped his bundle, realizing that he'd been caught in the act of stealing. His wizened face dropped. He raised his old, gnarled fingers to cover his eyes. As I watched, mesmerized, the old man began to stolidly weep. I winced in sympathy. I raised my hand protectively, as if to say, No, no, please, you don't need to cry. We're almost the same age, my friend, I wanted to say. How did you come to this, dear friend?

It was my first expression of cruise line chaplaining, although from a distance, granted. After so many years as a pastor at home, I recognized a look like that old man's, with desperate eyes that anticipate judgment. The look is universal. I've spent my whole pastoral life trying to reassure the frightened soul that stoically awaits God's inevitable wrath. A thought crossed my mind out of nowhere. *This is why you are here.* Was that a word from the Lord or my own imagination?

Impulsively, I called to the old man that we would get him what he needed, for clearly, he was in some kind of bitter need. Unfortunately, by calling to him I brought attention on him. I considered running back down the gangway to assist the old man but prayed where I stood. "Be not afraid," I prayed for him aloud. "Be not afraid."

A shout snatched my notice.

"You think you're going somewhere?" screamed a male crew member who was coordinating supplies on the pier. The overseer moved with large steps from his wooden pallets to push the hapless old man fleeing the vessel. The elderly man crumpled to his knees. "Get up! I said, get up! You belong below decks! How about I send you back to the witches' market in La Paz? You want to sell dog teeth again?"

"No, no, have mercy!"

The crew worker seized the elderly man under his arms to stand him up, turned him roughly by the shoulders, and shoved him repeatedly in the small of his back, through the door that was the crew's entrance. He then kicked the old man's sack into the seawater.

As he returned to his pallets, the supervisor noticed my shocked stare. He looked up at me. He planted his feet in defiance and placed both his hands onto his slender hips. Like a prison guard's, his eyes narrowed into a confrontational gaze. But his voice softened into a false friendliness, with a tone of bemusement. "These new employees from Bolivia! We have the worst trouble training them. Enjoy your journey!"

I rushed back to the atrium. The acidic taste of misgivings coated my tongue.

Was I really about to serve as an agent of God's love on a mysterious pleasure cruise? And who exactly was going to have pleasure? The ship appeared almost empty of guests. Did all cruises begin in this way? I wanted to grab my wife's hand and get her off of the *Grand Rapina* as fast as possible. "Sorry, it didn't work out," I would say. But Candace would reply, "James, my dear, there is no home anymore. We sold it."

Like the conquistador Hernán Cortés, who burned his ships upon landing in Mexico, for Candy and me, there was no way to return to our old way of living.

Through a window, I looked down quayside one last time. Now, no supplies were piled for loading, no officious crew members paced. Nothing moved except the gurgling water grazing against the ship's bow. I felt the contrast between the high, conditioned air circulating above me in the glittering aerie and the low, common air rolling densely across the humid pier. The thunderstorm that I'd feared in the downtown market was still on its way.

Shortly, the passenger gangway would be removed, and the ship's main door sealed. The crew would bring in the lines and hoist the harbor pilot flag. We would set sail. I felt my blood pressure rise at the thought. I remembered forlornly that I could have been home safely planting springtime bulbs.

As I make my statement here for the authorities, I can say that already I knew all would not be well on the *Grand Rapina*. Several decades of a pastor's discernment informed my opinion.

Let me keep going. I have much to say.

I want to tell everything.

CHAPTER THREE

With an ominous anticipation of what was to come, I returned to stand by my wife at the mermaid fountain. Its gushing jets coursed upward with a mist that put a chilling sprinkle on my clerical collar. I noticed that Candy's shoulders were slightly damp, too, and the water seemed to me an undesired christening into the *Grand Rapina*'s mission, whatever that might be. The violet light cast by the mermaid's lasers made my spouse's face seem subtly blanched. My wife's sickening color matched my mood.

"Did you have your last look?" Candace teased, not realizing that she probed an emotional wound. "Why so glum, James? You'd think we were about to cruise to hell. Come on, let's go find our stateroom." My wife tugged at my hand. "Did you surprise me with a bon voyage fruit basket?"

I didn't say a word. At certain moments in my life, I keep quiet and don't reveal everything that I know. I used to remember the Latin for it, but here's what the Stoic philosopher Cato said in translation: "I begin to speak only when I'm certain what I'll say isn't better left unsaid." Some people would not consider keeping silent unusual for a pastor, a person who, by calling, is sworn to keep the flock's sins and heartaches confidential. My introvert's personality has always assisted me in offering discreet counseling to the Christian sheep, and I've never been one to have the faintest desire to gossip.

This ability to hold my tongue has served me well in many difficult situations, such as at funerals. Whenever I've been asked by a family to say something commemorative about their deceased relative, I haven't thought that emphasizing the finer accomplishments of a person's life betrays the pastor's office. Not revealing everything that I think I know about a soul's eternal fate can be a gesture of common decency for a grieving family, while also helping me to avoid emotionally fraught, theologically debatable pronouncements at fragile social gatherings. If I consent to be the pastor at a funeral, even for someone who is not a church member, I should strive to be magnanimous, and I always have been.

After all, who really knows a human heart except God? Who can predict, with certainty, another person's eternal destination? I might believe that the ribald cad I am asked to bury is roasting on one of Hades' hottest spits, when the knave might have thrown himself on the Lord's mercy in the last five seconds of his wastrel life. And if I should ever meet this man strolling placidly on the golden bricks of heaven's trails, I don't think that I will even be particularly shocked, assuming I'm admitted myself. We serve a great God! He can redeem anyone. The Lord knows that in my own life, at times he has not had very much to work with, either, so far be it from me to sit in judgment of another.

Similarly, after witnessing the incident with the foreign worker on the dock, I decided to keep my misgivings about the *Grand Rapina* to myself for a while. For the foreseeable future, I would have to protect my wife from what I perceived as a dangerous reality. I would not confide my fears to her about our upcoming journey through Latin America. I would share those anxieties only with God through prayer. With my personal worries, I would remain silent. I would shoulder my cares alone. Candace was aboard the ship because of me, and only because of me, and I wanted her to have whatever joy she could glean from the trip, without my spoiling it for her with trepidations.

Part of my restraint in talking to Candy was my emotional evolution. Not only did I not want to make my wife afraid, but I think that I had begun to grapple maturely with what a dream that has been achieved looks like, as opposed to an aspiration. I had become a cruise ship chaplain, fulfilling a goal. The fact was, I had applied for a job and I'd gotten it, but it was not everything that I'd hoped it would be. In fact, it was a suspicious appointment and was scaring me. I saw that in future years I would have to search for my true motivations for uprooting my life. I had always thought that I had a high degree of self-knowledge, but apparently that was not the case, for as I stood on the *Grand Rapina*, I could not for the life of me explain why I'd chosen to be there. Hadn't I started out wanting to emulate Saint Paul? Hadn't I sensed a call to minister at sea? Now, all I could think about was how we were going to get through this ordeal.

So, rather than meet my wife's enthusiasm about our voyage with the alarming words "Stop the sale of our home right now," I responded to Candy with a calm request for a delay. I wanted more time in concentrated solitude to try to figure out how to extricate ourselves from our seafaring dilemma. It took all of the little bit of artifice that I possess to make a seemingly innocuous, off-hand remark to Candace, as I consciously decided to deceive my life's partner, although for her own welfare. Previously, I would never have dared to attempt such a transgression. Candace knew every curve and cranny of my heart, but now I had to lie to her, and convincingly.

As I strategized, the laser lights on the trollup mermaid changed color, and they startled me with their lewd illumination. That sultry female fish would not go away! She was interjecting her erotic presence into the important thoughts I had to think. I turned away from the legendary bustiness and spoke to my wife in as natural a tone of voice as I could muster. The best thing to do was to go through the motions of normalcy.

"I think I'll introduce myself to the Captain and staff, just to let them know I'm available anytime. You go find our room and get some lunch. I'll be along." I hoped that I sounded nonchalant.

Candace turned from primping in her compact mirror and clasped my wrist. Her eyebrows furrowed tensely. "James, sweetheart, I've been married to you for thirty-five years. What's the matter? We just got here. Why do you suddenly want to be alone?" Candy would not be so easy to fool.

I refolded the ship's map, keeping my eyes looking down, knowing that my wife would see through them to the bottom of my soul, if I let her. "People need to meet the chaplain right away, in case something happens. Let me take care of this. It won't take much time. I'll get off to a good start."

"I'll come with you. We can explore the ship together."

I had to be firm. "Not right now." I kissed my wife decisively on her forehead and guided her to a crew member. "Hello, I'm James Atterley. I'm the new ship's chaplain. Would you please show my wife to our stateroom while I introduce myself around?"

"Right away, Pastor. We're so glad to have you with us," the young man replied.

Candace looked at me with the resignation born of knowing her partner's stubbornness. She let herself be handed off. My wife had never been a pushover, and I knew that she was capable of disagreeing vehemently. But this time, she didn't. "Oh, all right. Meet me in our room in about an hour. I don't want to go to lunch without you, though, James. Why would I want to do that? Don't take too long."

"I'll be right there. Go get settled in. Here, you take the card key."

With that, I watched as Candy was whisked away. My throat tightened painfully at the separation, but I knew that I needed to scheme in solitude. As I stood alone, considering how to present subterfuge as truth, two long blasts of the ship's horn signaled that the *Grand Rapina* was leaving her berth. The vessel would not look back as she sailed her 90,000 tons through the jetties in Charleston Harbor, through the sea channel that leads to the ocean, and out to the open Atlantic waters.

I was committed to cruising, misgivings or not.

Through necessity, I began to play a long charade.

I reopened the ship's map. I traced my finger along its creases to examine the vessel's layout. If I had to stay, I would have to work, and work required my best efforts, or at least that appearance. I would have to trust that God would somehow redeem this retirement misstep, if that's what it was, and help me to be authentically useful while I was obligated to be onboard. I no longer expected to feel much happiness in our seafaring journey, but I did intend to fulfill my responsibilities until I could think of a way to recant my acceptance.

As a practical solution, perhaps Candy and I could arrange to go home at the first port of call. I ruminated over what kind of excuse I could give to Majestic Waves for my resignation, and my conscience smarted at the prospect of lying about a sudden illness. What could I do? I couldn't say that I'd decided to go home because I thought the trip had been misrepresented to me. It would be impossible to prove that accusation. I hoped to be able to resign online or over the phone, because if I had to do it in person, I was sure that I would flush magenta and have to invent even more lies to explain the change in my complexion. "See, this is part of my sickness," I would fib. "I'm blushing uncontrollably."

As I look back now, having been brought to account, I am struck by how bad I felt at telling such small falsehoods. Before joining the *Grand Rapina*, everything honorable in me was repulsed by lies, with no exceptions. I had spent my life in service to the truth, God's truth. On this voyage, I came to lie with some real talent for it, and without regret, because I had to, to resist enemies hellbent on destroying me. Now, I don't even recognize my lies as sins, but only as reactions to duress. I hope that the authorities feel the same way.

I continued to plot. For example, once we were extricated from the cruise line, probably in the middle of Central America, there were other problems, such as how my wife and I were supposed to find transport home. It would be at our own expense. And where would we stay in the meantime in a country unfamiliar to us? In this emergency, I could call the synod or missionary friends, most of whom would be knowledgeable about how to quickly depart from a foreign country. There was always the American embassy. Maybe a nearby American military installation could help us. At worst, we might have to endure a few days in uncomfortable housing before making our way back to South Carolina. We would go home exhausted, poorer, and crestfallen, but we would be safely home. I vowed to spend more time in prayer to strengthen my powers of discernment, so as to never find myself in this spot again.

Although what I wanted most was to have privacy to think about how to escape, I really did have to acquaint myself with the ship and my duties. The more that I learned, the more information I would have at my disposal to help my wife and me to get off of the cruise ship. In that frame of mind, I decided to explore the *Grand Rapina*. I had the notion that gathered information would translate into ammunition, and I had to do my job in the short-term, especially if someone really needed me. My willingness to stay was now contrived, but my pastor's heart for helping people was authentic.

I started exploring the cruise ship and investigating my job's duties from the top on down. I determined that first I would visit the ship's bridge. I knew nothing about that august locale, except for the usual reading of seafaring literature while in college. Herman Melville's *Moby Dick* came to mind, through which I had learned the common tropes about a hallowed nerve center peopled by shrewd and crusty men whose veins rushed with saltwater. On the *Grand Rapina*, would I find an old, hoary, barrel-chested sea captain overseeing a clutch of grizzled, hard-living mariners? Would they be engrossed in busily scribbling pencil marks on the well-worn vellum charts that would steer us expeditiously toward our first stop, the Port of Colon, Panama?

Probably not. Judging by the ship's state-of-the-art technology, I was more likely to encounter a version of Captain Kirk and Mr. Spock, if anything, and not Captain Ahab and Starbuck. I wondered if the *Grand Rapina*'s Captain realized that for all of its impressive beauty and technical wizardry, his vessel effused an atmosphere of oppression, at least for me. My instincts were leading me to sense that something terribly wrong was occurring with the unfolding journey. I was a novice at cruising but not at living, and I drew on my many years of well-developed intuition to posit that the *Grand Rapina* was not what she claimed to be. The problem remaining to be solved: What *was* she?

I continued to plan how to cope. I decided that after meeting the master of the vessel on the bridge, it would be prudent for me to stop by the infirmary to meet the ship's doctor. I expected to have more interaction with the physician than with the Captain, for cruise passengers, like parishioners, are always bruising themselves in the physical world, followed inevitably by doing damage to something spiritual. In my experience, one followed the other as night follows day. Both can be difficult to heal.

The doctor and I would commiserate. We would talk shop. I would take comfort in the doctor's fellowship until I could get off of the hideous boat, for I have always felt a kinship with caregivers. Like pastors, doctors are entrusted with the means of preservation and healing, just in different ways. Perhaps if I had developed a special fondness for the writings of Saint Luke, a doctor, instead of for Saint Paul, a mystical wanderer, I would not have found myself in this predicament on the *Grand Rapina*. In any event, I would present myself to the ship's doctor as a potential friend, and I would be up for any of his or her advice and enlightenment, except for a tour of the morgue.

Next, I would look up the ship's safety officer. After all, should anything go wrong on board the *Grand Rapina*, such as an explosion, God forbid, it would be the safety officer who would manage the crisis. It would be good for me to introduce myself to this person to make his acquaintance, if only to be able to recognize the face of the one to whom I should turn in the midst of an inferno. He (or she) would know where the most viable escape hatches were, which staircases to use, and when to lower the lifeboats.

Just thinking of those things made me cringe. Why wasn't I at home painting my garden shed? In the confusion of a catastrophe, and with so few crew apparently manning the *Grand Rapina*, I did not want to have to rely on my ability to study the hard copy of the ship's map to get myself and Candace to safety. I did not even know how to put on a life vest. It seemed essential to have that private lesson. Would there be safety drills?

After some reflection and spending some time in seclusion, curiously, I started to feel a little better. Planning was calming me. I even felt that I was getting a handle on the situation. Nothing would take me by surprise, I believed. I remembered that in a short time I would enjoy a good meal. Now there was a much-needed, encouraging thought. Would they have grilled swordfish tonight? I felt my emotions settle down. Perhaps my intuition about this journey was all wrong, I second-guessed. I knew that I was with a reputable cruise line, and I trusted that God would order my steps. That's what the Christian walk is all about, belief undergirded by faith, even in perilous circumstances.

More or less certain, then, that God had called me to this work on the *Grand Rapina*, but in a way yet to be revealed to me, I watched the decks zip by on the glass elevator up to the bridge and enjoyed the ascending views. I even began to hum an old hymn. My natural inclination is toward optimism. How bad could everything be? I think that I actually wanted to salvage my good feelings about joining the *Grand Rapina*. A part of me wanted to fit in with the other professionals and redeem the voyage. I became almost cheerful.

The elevator lurched to a gentle stop. As I stepped out, I saw that I was at the very top of the ship, and toward the center of the bow, with a commanding vista that was accentuated by angled, floor-to-ceiling glass panes. These windows shimmered with a near-blinding sheen. The Atlantic Ocean lay before me in CinemaScope breadth. I could see the blue waves for miles and miles in the distance, languorously folding over themselves and tumbling into misty etchings, sending their sharp spray in all directions. Despite my being indoors, the smell of salt filled my nostrils with a tangy sting. For the first time, I also felt in my stomach the almost imperceptible roll of the ship, a feeling that I would come to recognize as a harbinger of seasickness. I made a mental note to get pills for motion sickness from the medical center.

It was hard not to be dazzled by the *Grand Rapina*. I found that I enjoyed her spectacular accoutrements, and a sense of satisfaction at our affiliation spread through me. I was privileged to be onboard. I was one of the upper crust now. I thought that my résumé must have impressed Majestic Waves Cruises, since I had beaten out so many other applicants. I wondered what it was about me that had made the difference. Could it have been the sample sermon that I'd recorded and included with my application? I have to admit that I do have a real gift for dramatic readings.

Maybe it was something else. Could it have been that Reverend Carter wrote such a glowing recommendation that the cruise line found it impossible to pass me up? Matilda and I went way back. We'd gone to seminary together. She'd always noted my particular aptitude for eschatology, and perhaps she'd mentioned that strength in her letter to Majestic Waves. Perhaps she'd highlighted my winning ways with new church members. And my humility. I never considered it beneath me to put on the coffee pot. Perhaps Matilda had mentioned the many times that she'd seen me steady at the bedside of the dying, or the great results that I always got for the coffers with my sensitive and moving annual sermon on tithes.

I thought that there were so many factors that distinguished my background, it was really no surprise at all that I'd been chosen as the new chaplain for the *Grand Rapina*. It was inevitable, I was so well-qualified. In fact, the more that I thought about it, it looked like I was in the center of God's will, and I should not be too self-effacing about having received such a big, splashy call. Not only *could* it have been me, but it *was* me who was chosen as the new ship's chaplain, and I looked forward to serving on the *Grand Rapina* for many years. What a good fit!

Gazing around outside the elevator, I walked to a sign that read "RESTRICTED ACCESS." Honestly, I never gave it a second thought. The sign seemed to be printed for other people. The Captain and his staff were just beyond a door, and it was my mission to meet them. I knocked and entered the inner sanctum of the vessel. I learned later that the bridge on the *Grand Rapina* was 130 feet wide, from port to starboard, and that it even expanded over the sides of the ship to enable the staff to have a wide view of the vessel. The Captain's control was thus expansive. His knowledge of his ship was all-seeing.

After passing through the designated doorway, I prepared to take my place among the leaders. This room was where the action happened. I looked good. I felt good, too. I began my visit by making an announcement, as if I were the emcee for the afternoon performance of sail craft.

I lifted my arms in oratory. "Gentleman, I don't mean to interrupt," I said to the mariners huddled at their stations. "I just want to let you know that I'm here, according to my job offer. I'm Pastor James Atterley, the new ship's chaplain. I don't mean to complain, but no one has told me where to report. Is there some kind of an orientation?" I grinned self-consciously and rather ridiculously pulled my job contract out of my shirt pocket and flipped it open like a policeman's badge, as evidence of my legitimacy. My nervousness was showing. I look back on the whole thing now and am profoundly embarrassed.

I think that spectacle was my response to being over-awed. As a pastor, I'm accustomed to public speaking, and so I just stood there and talked, trying to fit in, assuming that people would listen. Everyone had always listened in the past, at church, and I reverted to using a familiar skill. I intended to demonstrate a light touch of employee initiative. I didn't know what else to do. In any other job, someone would have served as my guide, such as a senior pastor or a human resources representative. With this job, I had simply been told when and where to show up. Thinking about it now, I see that this was another clue that the *Grand Rapina* was suspiciously odd.

"Who had the hell to let *you* in?" the tallest among the officers bellowed in broken English. He looked Scandinavian, pale and stern. Beside him, the man who had greeted me so cryptically in the atrium also scowled. "Padre, can you not read the signage?" he said gruffly. "You are breaching our security. I should have you taken away."

I offered an attempt at disarming humor. I pointed to that sign posted above the door. "Well, God is not subject to 'RESTRICTED ACCESS,'" I joked. Then, I paused, the gravity of my infraction starting to sink in. I realized that I'd committed a sin of chain-of-command. I did not belong in the bridge at all. I wanted to crawl under the boat. "I'm sorry, I meant no harm."

A somber man wearing the gold-striped, four-bar epaulettes glared up from his computer screen directly at me. He was visibly angry at having been distracted, and by a peasant. Pomaded, wearing a silver ring on an index finger, and stylishly outfitted in his tailored navy suit jacket, the Captain had artistic, delicate hands and an imperious, czarist tone. The wrinkles in his face spoke to years of experience navigating on the high seas. He probably knew exactly what was in Davy Jones' locker. This Captain stared at me from over his electronic navigational charts and issued an authoritative notice.

"I am Captain Moze Balodis, and you are out of place," came the rebuke in a Baltic voice. "Pastor, I will make time for you later. Although you are not aware, I am presently disembarking our harbor pilot, a complicated task in this gathering storm. Please, no more conversation. You are dismissed." The Captain returned his attention to the encroaching fog bank outside. "Slow to eight knots!" he commanded his staff. Picking up his radiotelephone, he barked more instructions to the officer escort on deck. "Shine a light forward, in case Captain Jacobs should fall from the ladder!"

I stood rebuffed, feeling scolded and publicly chastened. I felt my stomach tense, and not because of the ship's roll. I'd been treated like a boy with a sucker stuck in his hair. After feeling embarrassment, I felt outrage. How dare such a man scold me, a representative of God and his elder in both age and education! I began to stammer a retort, but instead, flustered, with my hands sweating, I made a hasty exit through the sacred, special door.

Once alone, I leaned unsteadily against a deck railing, seething with an anger that felt like flames on my flesh. My vulnerabilities began to flood my mind. He would not have spoken to me that way if I weren't so old, I thought. I am a fellow executive! I fumed. I stewed a bit more and hurried toward the elevator. I had every right to be on the bridge, I justified.

The more that I ruminated about the incident, the more that I felt insulted. My thoughts raced. Did they think that I'm a mind reader? I asked myself. Why hadn't they bothered to plan my first day as the chaplain? How was I supposed to know they were worried about the incoming fog? Would I have been so easily dismissed if I had been wearing a construction worker's hard hat and not a minister's clerical collar? Are church duties light? Don't most men run from staring into the mouth of a grave and lending solace to mourners? How dare any men, especially filthy sailors, patronize my religious calling!

I was a pious person and I wanted, always, to do the right thing. The Captain and his staff could have welcomed me onto the bridge, forgiven my awkwardness, and overlooked such a small social mistake, knowing that I was trying to find my way. They could have made me one of them, drawn me in as a part of their team. Instead, they kicked me out of their precious, magical space. How was I ever going to work with such inconsiderate brutes?

Riding down in the elevator, I ignored the churning, foaming views that had entertained me before, because rising up on the horizon in front of my eyes like a windswept kite was my own tattered, reeling pride. I had gone from wanting to abandon the whole cruise to desperately wanting to be a part of it. Not a very auspicious beginning, I grieved. I had thought that I had more of a managerial presence. I wondered if I, as a seventy-two-year-old-man, really should be at home in my recliner, not on the *Grand Rapina*. What had ever made me think that I could be adventurous like Saint Paul? Had I taken leave of my senses? Only a few months ago, I couldn't even remember the Lord's Prayer!

A full hour passed before I could compose myself. I rubbed my eyes in consternation. Had I really waved my contract at them? I labored mightily to put my ego aside. It was throbbing as if beaten with a stick. I had to admit that I had gone into the most secure, elite area on the vessel without permission, believing that I would be seen as the officers' equal, even though they had never set eyes on me before. In my arrogance, I had thought that I would be instantly accepted into an inner circle, one I had claimed to want nothing to do with only minutes earlier, and I was humiliated when I was summarily asked to leave.

That's what had happened to me. I had to take frank stock. When surrounded by the onboard aristocrats, I had discovered that I was attracted to power. I couldn't be offended out of all proportion, I reflected. I had been in the wrong. I considered who I really was. I work for God, you see. I am not God. His glory precedes him, and nothing is kept from him, but I have no glory at all. "Pride goeth before destruction," I quoted to myself. I walked pensively to my stateroom to check in with my own pilot, the Lord. I knew that he would not reject me.

On the way, I noticed strange things around me, everywhere. The ship seemed to be shutting down instead of rousing itself for a fresh onslaught of gleeful vacationers. As I walked by the dance floor, I saw that the overhead strobe lights were completely dark. A worker stood on a ladder, unscrewing them. The slot machines in the casino were draped in cloths that hung like shrouds. The crew had not even bothered to open the jewelry store. The photographer's studio where passengers were invited to pose in their stylish resort attire was unmanned and shuttered. Why were these entertainments unneeded?

I kept walking, confused by this cruise, but then I cried out. I recoiled in horror. In an alcove next to the casino, a bloody needle and vial had been flung into a potted tropical vine. They dripped onto the carpet in a thick crimson puddle, blotting out the gold starburst pattern. This mayhem suggested to me that there were those aboard who knew that soon it would be pointless to try to hide the ship's true mission, so why be coy about it? Blood would soon be horrifyingly, sloppily, casually, on tap. I covered my mouth to hold in a gasp. I tried to look away but stared all the more as a lizard hopped out of the flowerpot, covered in a red ooze. With my eyes widening, my footsteps dashed away from the carnage. I realized that I'd dropped the job contract that I was so proud of. When I stole a glance backward to find it, I saw that the letter was covered in bloody lizard tracks.

I grabbed a painting bolted to a wall with both hands to steady myself. Then and there I returned to my first, most accurate, suspicions about the *Grand Rapina*. My initial impression was true, then. This ship was a barge of the Devil, a rogue cruise liner. The realization terrified me, but strangely, it also absolved me, emotionally, of my gaffes with the officers. What of it if I had gone onto the bridge? I rationalized that anybody would have been awkward on such a cruise, given the circumstances, because I was in the grip of a superior force and not fully able to defend myself.

Thereafter, I moderated my ownership of personal culpability on the voyage, in big things and small. In this fallen world, it does not pay to feel unnecessarily guilty. The righteous soul must be able to assert its innocence, and even to wield the sword, to avoid being consumed by evil. Must we turn the other cheek, even to the point of consenting to our own murder? I think not.

If I was guilty of doing anything morally wrong on the *Grand Rapina*, it was because I was trying to help myself and others to survive a close encounter with evil. Often as the voyage deteriorated, I felt that there was no good choice to be made, only a course to implement from among varying degrees of terror.

As I write this statement prior to my trial, I'm struck by how guileless I originally was.

I was trying to keep my sanity. I had to learn to be brave.

That is what I will tell my judges.

* * *

As Candace made her way to a staircase with the crew worker, she looked wistfully at James as he left, consumed with his duty. *If only he could relax a little*, she thought. *He's a good man, but he never stops working.* "I hope our stateroom has a deck up high enough for a great view of the waves. It's really all about seeing the water, isn't it?"

"Yes, the water," the young man nodded. "Some people are afraid of the sea, but not me. Where I come from, we worship it."

"What's your home country?" Candace asked brightly.

"Greece."

"You're Greek, but you don't have an accent."

"My mother was from Los Angeles. I spent a lot of time there."

"Oh, the City of Angels," Candace said. "A wonderful name for a wonderful place."

"Yes, my mom said I was born with an angel in the room."

In all of her years, Candace had never heard such an assertion. "You mean, like a prophet?"

"Well, kind of," the crew member replied. "But my mother never said whether it was a good angel or a bad angel." The room steward looked over his shoulder at Candace. "Apparently, it could've gone either way."

Candace walked more slowly behind the young man, keeping her distance.

"Here we are, Mrs. Atterley, your very own stateroom." The crew worker shoved the electronic boarding pass into the door and swung it open. "Good-bye, until we meet again very soon." The steward smiled with his lips but not with his eyes. He returned Candace's room pass to her. He seemed to know more than the older woman about upcoming shipboard reunions.

Candace was uncomfortable but unable to pinpoint just why. The light hair on her arms rose wispily. She remained non-committal about ever seeing that weird young man again. "It's a big ship. We might not run into each other anymore."

The young steward leaned forward, directly into Candace's face. "I will never go away. I've been assigned to you," he whispered. "And maybe my angel's still with me." The crew member gave Candace a salute and backed down the hallway with a formal, military air.

Candace stepped quickly into her stateroom, closing the door between herself and the steward as fast as possible. She leaned against it, shaking. She took several deep breaths to calm her nerves. She looked inside the suite. Her suitcases had been delivered. Candace tore the pink one open, tossing clothes all over the room, rummaging, searching for her favorite summer sweater. She wrapped it tightly around her. *That man had the coldest presence. I felt it in my bones. James is going to think I'm exaggerating, but I know what I felt.*

* * *

Just off of the stateroom's balcony, thrashing far from sight in the whirring currents of the ocean Candace had wanted to be near, ravenous sharks swarmed in the cruise liner's wake, eagerly awaiting the first dinner's refuse. Like demons of the deep, the prescient sharks knew exactly what to expect of this seagoing vessel. Without regard for strict maritime regulations, meat and blood would soon be plentiful for gorging upon, the sharks knew, when the ship illegally dumped its garbage at sea.

"That old lady ain't gonna last a week," Chris Adamos, descended from the gangs of Los Angeles, sneered, abandoning the accent that he used with the ritzy people. He stepped out of the crew members' elevator and into the ship's main corridor. "That old lady gonna be 'Shark Candy.'"

CHAPTER FOUR

I struggled to contain my apprehension when Candace opened the door to our state room. I wanted to scream out that there was blood all over the floor downstairs, but I didn't. I was talking to my wife, not a detective on an investigation, so I kept my accusations about the *Grand Rapina* to myself, despite some internal wrestling. Although Candy was my life's confidante, I couldn't bring up the true nature of the cruise ship, I just couldn't do it, not yet, because I couldn't stand to bring fear to my wife.

The authorities might see my withholding of such horrific information as a type of negligent denial about it, an actual disservice to my wife, as well as to the few innocent members of the crew, who should have been made aware of the dangers. The psychologists might believe that I had a break from reality from this point forward, and that I blocked the significance of what I'd seen from my conscious awareness. After all, they might say, most people would have mentioned it if they had seen "a lizard dripping blood, crawling on their credentials." My ministerial friends might wonder how I encountered what I believed to be evil and yet said nothing. All of these onlookers might think that my not wanting to scare my wife was not a good enough reason to stay quiet.

I don't know why I said nothing at first. I can only say that maybe, under pressure, I learned that I was just a gardener, an old man who pulls weeds, not a hero. I wasn't confident enough to assert that evil was afoot, not yet. On some level, I might not have wanted to get involved, might have thought it was not my task. And I certainly wasn't prepared for God to ask anything hard of me. I'd only wanted light (but honorable) duties onboard the *Grand Rapina*.

At our cabin's door, my spouse greeted me with a lingering kiss and clung to me in the threshold, before I was even inside of our stateroom.

Candace seemed to have missed me very much and was especially eager to have my company. I'd only been away for a little while, but my wife met me as if I were coming back from a blazing battlefield. I was pleasantly startled by her ardor. Memories began to flood my mind. The Candace holding me was the same one who had once been much more than a lunch date; indeed, she was the one who had so infatuated me that I took the biggest chance of my life and committed to her and gave myself to her and everything that I owned and would ever own, to her.

Candy's body was still slim and the nape of her neck, still soft. A sweet recollection of our time as young lovers filled my thoughts as I tenderly held my wife. Ah, those were the years! For a few fleeting moments, we were impoverished, twenty-six-year-old college students again — she in nurse's training and me in seminary — two earnest souls newly embarked on life's quest with not much more in assets between us than a box of spaghetti noodles.

There in the doorway, my youthful masculinity was briefly restored in an impulse to protect Candy and shield her from anything that might ever cause her harm. No, I would not tell her about the bloody syringe. For a moment, I remembered the passion that could have slayed any dragon for my lady, and had, in fact, resulted in sweaty sins that I had self-consciously confessed to my most trusted spiritual advisor. "Saint Augustine would understand . . . " I had nervously whispered to Pastor Hal, as red-faced as if I had been caught in the act.

As we held each other there in the stateroom's doorway, I felt sure that Candy remembered, too, but that, as a nurse, being more realistic, perhaps, about the fleshly demands and inevitable outcomes of mortal physiology, she experienced less guilt than I ever would. For a few moments, once more we were not old, not afflicted, not weary, not burdened. We were young again as before, rosy, radiant, just starting out, counting on each other, there in that doorway. Then, suddenly, we were not.

"James, what took you so long?" my wife cooed softly in my ear.

"I'm here now, sweetheart, I'm here."

I stepped inside the cruise suite. Invisible helping hands had placed our luggage in our cabin. The helpers might have been magicians, for the bags had disappeared at the dock, turned into mist for a while, apparently, and then materialized again with their Samsonite logo, in our room, as if they'd never been hidden in the metaphysical plane at all. I came to see these appearances and disappearances as symptomatic of the whole cruise trip. Nothing was what it seemed. Materializing and dematerializing luggage was just the start. Everything onboard the *Grand Rapina* was so disorienting; for all I knew, my shaving kit had been to Mars and back.

Candy was unaccustomed to the perks of cruise ship travel, and I think that she must have discovered that when others do the heavy lifting, it can be quite enjoyable, at least for those escaping the chores. I hated to think that way about my wife, but there it is. From the evidence, it seemed that Candy enjoyed being waited on. That was my guess, judging by the haphazard way in which she'd flung her suitcases' contents around the stateroom, as if she'd already internalized that neatening and cleaning would fall to someone else. The suite looked as if it had been stirred.

This emergence of Marie Antoinette in Candace Atterley surprised me, for my wife was ordinarily a humble, self-reliant woman, not a haughty mistress who demanded that somebody empty the chamber pot. Had I been married to a repressed diva for all of these years? I didn't want to make too much of it, because it was only one incident, but I would have to object if Candy's new indifference to keeping tidy were the beginning of a trend. Still, I was not my wife's manager, and I didn't want to appear to supervise her or to appraise her in any way other than what a person who shared her marriage and her living space had a right to do.

I looked around disapprovingly at the mess strewn high and low. "It's a wonderful room, but it exploded," I said to my spouse, gathering up her shorts and tops and swimsuit from off the floor. Her sunhat had landed cock-eyed on a lamp, which made both of them teeter dangerously. Had there been an earthquake while I was out? "This isn't like you, Candy. You're careful with your clothes. What in the world went on in here?"

"I was cold and looking for my sweater. Too much air conditioning." Candy was now uncharacteristically laconic. She turned her back to me, which she never did. My wife developed a sudden interest in finding the light switch in the closet and walked away from me.

Bringing the fabric arms down neatly, laying one over the other carefully, I folded an embroidered blouse, frowning. "I see, just too cold.

Being cold makes you throw clothes." I thought that perhaps I had angered my wife more than I knew by sending her to our stateroom alone. It couldn't be that she'd thrown a belligerent fit in retaliation. After observing her for a few minutes, I noticed that Candy was gripping her temples. She used that gesture when she had the kaleidoscope aura of a migraine coming on, covering her eyes to ward off the sharp flashes of crystalline light.

Now, my conscience royally ached. I felt guilty about delaying my wife's lunch, because going without a meal commonly brought on her migraines. If I didn't take care of her promptly, I knew that Candace would be painfully incapacitated for hours, and at the very start of our trip, all because of me. I rummaged through Candy's toiletries for her pills, noticing that she had only three. I poured one tiny green square of relief into my palm, and twisted the bottle shut to protect the rest, for it would be impossible to get a refill while at sea. "I know what that means when you hold your head like that," I said to my wife. "Take this medication. We'll get it under control."

"Pull the shades down, will you, James?" Candace replied after sipping some water. She moved to the bed, slipping out of her sandals.

This situation was just one more consequence of my futile stroll around the ship. I had nothing to show my wife for my time apart from her — no interesting anecdote about the upcoming port and no room number of new friends we could meet for a cocktail. I had nothing except my humiliation on the bridge, which my ego concealed and I dared not mention, and the psychedelic memory of a bloody tableau next to an incongruously darkened gaming hall.

None of that was suitable for sharing with someone who seemed to have been alarmed at my absence, especially if that someone was suffering from an excruciating headache. The whole misbegotten exercise of spending time by myself had been a series of misfiring jolts. My time away from my wife hadn't been productive at all, unless it counted as an unwanted seminar in self-awareness, and it had had the unintended side effect of causing my closest loved one pain.

I did not mention my interactions with the staff at all, and Candy didn't ask me about them, either. Because of our long relationship, she trusted that I had been where I said I would go, and she seemed to have no curiosity about my explorations. Thank goodness, because if she had inquired I would have had to make up a story that left out the demeaning parts. I was sorry that Candy had gotten a migraine, and that I was probably the cause of it, but I was glad at her incuriosity. For me, it made things easier. I was so preoccupied that I never even thought to ask what she'd been up to in my absence.

"Can I get you another cold drink to help you feel better?"

"No, I just want to lie down for a while." Candy gathered up the little folded-towel swans placed on the bed by the cleaner and handed the birds to me. I hoped that the room steward hadn't worked too hard on them, because they didn't elicit even a smile from my wife. Candy zipped out of her clothes and pulled back the bedspread. She sat down on the edge of the mattress and gripped her forehead again. Then she crawled under the sheets, whimpering.

"What do you suppose brought on your migraine, my dearest?" I asked gingerly. I hoped for some exoneration. I didn't get it.

"Who knows? I don't want to talk about it."

That sounded final. Even with the shades drawn down, around their silken edges illumination still poured forth from the powerful sunshine bouncing off of the ocean. The light was so plentiful that restraining it would have been like trying to hold back a cascade of liquid mercury, virtually impossible. It spilled everywhere, making every crack and crease in the window shade glow. So, still able to see my way around in the dim cabin, I turned my attention to examining our new shipboard residence.

As a gardener, of course I first noticed the fresh snapdragons and stargazers that had been placed on the room's nightstands. Their fragrance was mild and familiar. I made a mental note not to knock these vases over in the middle of the night when I wanted a drink of the bottled water sitting next to them. On second thought, I moved the flowers to the small desk across the room, out of harm's way. Let's be honest. I would forget mid-reach, and splashed water and broken crockery would be the result.

In addition to flowers, another treat had been bestowed. I munched on the chocolate candies that had been left on a lacy paper doily for our enjoyment. Tasty; they had a smooth mango filling. There were six in all, shaped like stars, to coordinate with the stargazer flower theme, I supposed. Candy's headache would be made worse by the caffeine, so I ate them all. As a favor to her, of course.

Though the stateroom was cramped by American standards, it was adequate, and its neutral color scheme of tans and creams with ocean-blue accents emanated an air of quietude. Unfortunately, it didn't take long for me to experience the discomfiture of discovering that nearly everything was nailed down. I appreciated the wisdom of making sure that furniture would not fly around in a gale, but I wasn't much comforted by it, and I thought that it would be small reassurance if I ever really found myself tossed about in a typhoon. In that event, I would've preferred to get off of the ship entirely to rush to dry land, where all of the furnishings are impetuously mobile, and take my chances with them. I needed more to feel safe at sea than an immovable dresser, especially on the *Grand Rapina*.

The stateroom contained a king-sized bed, a definite blessing, because my hip bursitis required that I have space enough to spread out. I saw that Candy was leaving plenty of room should I want to crawl in, and my conscience was pricked all over again. Four large feather pillows graced the quilted bedspread, with pillowcases that were fancily monogrammed with the ship's insignia. Two more pillows were tucked away neatly into a small closet that included a steam iron as big as a blacksmith's anvil, which Candace would never use, now that she was a queen. All mending and ironing would be sent out, doubtless. I chose the plumpest pillow as the one to put between my legs at night to ease my hips. I felt no guilt at all in taking it from my wife. I had a greater need.

The attached bathroom gave me immediate pause. Indeed, it was petite. When I stretched out both of my arms, I could touch every wall, except the one for the soap niches in the shower. The bathroom was so sturdy and durable that I thought it could be hosed down by a fire brigade in its entirety every twenty-four hours, instead of being sanitized piece by piece by the steward. The bathroom had the solidity of a nuclear bunker. It was invincible. There was no bath tub, which would be a problem for anyone wanting to shave her legs, which, thankfully, wasn't me.

Narrow rectangular mirrors were clamped above a shallow sink. These seemed designed by someone who had never cared to see his visage. The miniscule mirrors made it difficult for me to peer at more than a third of my face at a time, and only then if I tilted my head up and down in precise degrees. Clipping my beard would be a precarious escapade. I would have to mind the scissors and note well the location of my jugular. Plus, I would have to try hard not to be poked in the eye by the towel hook, which was placed dangerously close to the mirrors by quixotic people who apparently wanted to ensure that I wasn't frigidly wet for too long but that I remained, inexplicably, unshaven.

Then there was the toilet. It was a beast out of legend. The first time that I used it, it roared like a sea monster just harpooned. I had to check to make sure that all of my private parts were still attached when I stood up, so fierce was the toilet's suction. One would certainly not want to fall inside, for limbs and digits would be expendable, and if anything were misplaced in the bowl, such as a cuff link or a tie clip, it would have to be considered an offering to the ocean imp. I put my reading glasses on a chain, just in case I ever had to reel them in.

The miniature bathroom contained all of the fixtures necessary to perpetuate good health and civilization, I supposed. But I came to have my doubts about it later, once Candace had told me that the water used to scrub the ship's decks is actually recycled toilet, shower, and sink water that is collected daily from the passengers and stored in bacteria-treated tanks in the belly of the vessel. I would be required to put my faith in microbiology's ability to prevent a reunion with everybody's mortal ablutions in a virulent, possibly fatal, format. It is best not to know some things, I'm afraid.

I continued to walk around the cabin, opening cubbies and lifting lids. I came across the room safe and couldn't resist fiddling with it for a few minutes as Candace dozed. I had no earthly possessions to put inside the safe, except for my wedding ring, which I never took off. I knew that if I weren't careful, though, Candy would feel compelled to use the safe once she found it, even if just to put her own wedding rings inside, and hysterical, catastrophic loss would unfold when she couldn't get the thing open.

To prevent that eventuality, I took out the laminated card that explained how to create a combination for the lock. I would learn to set the safe, and we would be safe. I picked three numbers that corresponded to our wedding anniversary. My memory wasn't what it used to be, so I had to choose the numbers carefully and rely on those associated with an indelible date in my mind.

No luck. I tried to unlock that safe over and over. It was maddening. I found that I could remember the numbers, all right, but not when to turn the dial to the right or left. To prevent future problems that would require a blowtorch to resolve, I placed a chair strategically in front of the safe to hide it and its complicated watch works from Candy. Last time I checked, it was still locked.

The television was mounted on the wall at the foot of the bed. The screen wasn't overly large, but it would do. I picked up the remote control and clicked through the channels, most of which pertained to onboard shopping, the climate of ports of call, and swimming safety. Only one show caught my eye: I thought that I might come back later for the wine-tasting class. A live webcam showed the sea in both forward and aft views. There was an entire channel devoted to maps of Latin America, but I could not find a single channel that showed basketball games. I saw that Majestic Waves Cruises had purchased the value internet plan for Candy and me, so I would not be able to stream movies, not that it mattered. Oh, well.

One interesting channel described all of the menu offerings available from room service. The channel included a breakfast menu, a daytime menu, and a late-night menu. Dishes had evocative names with Caribbean overtones, such as "Going Bananas Barbecue" and "Toucan Tango Tuna Salad." Very cute. The camera zoomed in on every dish, punctuating their appetizing qualities, and a soundtrack of something like rumba music was intended to make one salivate. Liquor and beer were available for delivery to staterooms, and cocktails could be brought as well, but they could not be taken out of the suite. How strange. Who would want to be confined to his cabin while enjoying his lemon drop martini? Not me. Cocktails make me sociable.

The star of the stateroom, of course, was the balcony. Majestic Waves Cruise Lines had generously placed us on one of the highest decks, and our view of the horizon was nothing less than sensational. The terrace seemed to float like a flying carpet, as the winds and waves sped by. Jutting out airborne just to the border of arousing fear-of-heights panic, the little balcony provided Candy and me with a quiet space for reading our morning devotions in the days that followed and made us especially aware of the firmament's elevated location far above our planet's coursing oceans. In this tranquil spot, not only our bodies, but also our hearts, were uplifted.

Once my wife's headache medicine had kicked in, she opened the door to the balcony where I lingered and beckoned me back indoors. The cold compress she'd put on her forehead had left a red rash on her skin in the raised-dot pattern of the wash cloth, which I hoped would subside shortly. Candy was refreshed, though. Thank God for pharmacology.

"You seem much better."

"Let's get back on track. I need some food," my wife said. "I haven't had a bite all day."

As I said, this issue was of my doing. The worst of it was that my wavering commitments had made Candy ill by depriving her of the food that she needed on a regular schedule, given her tendency toward migraines. I felt ashamed that I'd deprived her. I wanted to take her to a good restaurant right away.

Also, I began to be enticed by the luxurious surroundings and the prospect of what it would be like on the *Grand Rapina* if one were really an ordinary pensioner aboard on a much-deserved vacation. I was fast losing the feel of being an employee, of the *Grand Rapina* or of God. I wanted to enjoy myself fully and take advantage of every convenience and amenity, including those renowned eateries cruises are famous for. If Candace were becoming Marie Antoinette, I could easily turn into Louis XVI.

"We could have a nice meal brought in," I suggested. "I found the TV channel that runs the room service menu. Are you sure you wouldn't like to rest for another hour?"

"I bought new pink nail polish for our first day at sea."

"That's so nice, but you can do your nails tomorrow, when you feel better, don't you think?"

Candy ran her fingers through her short white hair, wrinkling her forehead. She reached for her hairbrush in her purse and primped. "I want to see the ship. My nails can wait, but let's go have a late lunch and look around." Before I knew it, my wife was putting on fresh Rhapsody lipstick. Candy used her handy compact for this, not the slivers of mirrors in the bathroom, and she pulled herself together in under ten minutes. "James, where did you put my seersucker slacks? I've told you a million times, don't touch my things! Did you move my sandals? I've asked you not to do that, remember? I put my hat right over there, where is it? When are you going to listen? You can't fool me, I know your ears still work."

Truthfully, I was heartened by Candy's criticism. It meant that she was feeling better, full of vim and vinegar. If my wife wanted to scold me for the rest of the afternoon, I'd have no problem with it at all and would bear the barrage with a smile. Lord, my girl could chatter! I was glad that she was up to it, and, secretly, I felt better when she felt better. In fact, for decades I had set my own temperament's thermostat according to my darling wife's.

I tried to make amends by taking Candace to the restaurant with the best reputation on the ship, according to our welcome folder. It was called "The Sky on Reserve." My wife and I believed that one of the great pleasures of life is enjoying a good meal, so we were off to investigate. I thought about putting on a sport coat, but then decided against it. At the last moment before leaving our cabin, Candace wanted once again to paint her fingernails for the occasion, but I managed to convince her otherwise.

The restaurant's theme was all about eating inside of the clouds. The seating rooms were cleverly decorated in a technique that encouraged the blue and white paints of the ceiling cum sky to gradually melt into the blue and white waves on the walls. The ethereal effect was more like dining inside of a soft and feathery cocoon rather than lounging among the clouds, but the impact was still surreal and entertaining. I noticed that a vapor of some kind seemed to be pumped through the air to imitate mists, and after my second martini at the bar, I had to resist the urge to lick my finger and twirl it in the air to check the direction of the winds.

The culinary staff must have been trained by fine artists, or folklorists, because we had never before seen the extravaganza of what could be done to a common watermelon. From out of the succulent flesh were coaxed three-dimensional faces of fairies, complete with ruby-rich, blushing cheekbones. The variegated greens and yellows in the melons' rinds lent definition to ears and eyes and teeth. The fruit seemed able to really smile, with a variety of expressions, too, from sly smirk to spritely joy. The fruit looked so lifelike that one might engage it in conversation and inquire why it was so gleeful and expect a reply, so realistic were the melons' fairy features.

Other culinary art forms also displayed delicate and advanced skills. Tall ice sculptures glimmered in the form of swans so intricately carved that Candace and I could count their feathers in the frost. Pastel petit fours, macaroons and madeleines, eight-layer cakes, bombes, tartes, charlottes, crepes, and lattice-top pies were dusted with authentic gold flakes. Tinctures had been mixed from the secrets of alchemists to tint the shimmering icings. Colorful spices were combined with the skill of painters, producing portraits of jaguars in turmeric, black mustard, and sesame seeds on canvases of white rice.

We took it all in. Butcher block carving stations for every kind of meat and fish, from steer to sturgeon, groaned under the weight of the juicy roasts, legs, shoulders, fins, and fowls that waited to be served with tantalizing, sumptuous sauces accompanied by sizzling mushrooms of many types and sizes, including the rarest of truffles. Large onions were sizzling on steel skewers so large they might have been swords. Other vegetables of every color, texture, and shape gave off their aromatic essence, and these were steamed, creamed, fried, baked, and poached. I thought that I would sample a little bit of everything.

Handcrafted loaves of organic bread ran the gamut from sweet to savory, and these were slung into elaborate loops, ropes, rolls, and crosses. Whipped cream was poured by the quart over green-capped, crimson strawberries. Rustic rounds of cheeses, both soft and firm, were flecked in spots of blue, orange, and yellow and piled high on tables draped in satin swaddling. Even the humble radish and baby apple garnishes were artfully shaved, ingeniously twisted, and finely pared into cascading facets like edible jewels. I had never before worried about succumbing to the sin of gluttony, but now I encountered its full power to overtake one into slavery.

Strangely, no other passengers were in the dining room. I wondered if Candace and I had gotten ahead of ourselves. Could we be walking in on a private affair? What if any second now a hundred guests rushed through the doors for their catered birthday party for their blind grandmother, and found my wife and me eating up the twice-baked potatoes? What if they discovered *their* gravy on *my* beard? What if Candace would have to put back her slice of coconut cake ingeniously tinted purple by the crushed snails imported from Italy to dye the frosting? Imagine taking that from her hands!

I preferred to think that our intrusion wasn't possible, and ascribed the absence of other guests in the dining room to our fortuitous timing. Somehow, we'd arrived between shifts, that's all. Thanks to selective memory, I'm sure, I recalled the Bible story in which the rich man gave a banquet and all of his invited guests declined, so he opened up his house to the poor and downtrodden to come and feast with him. Even if we weren't invited, then, perhaps charity would let us stay? That's not what the parable means, as I well knew, but it suited my own desire, which was to dive into the chafing dishes and not look back, with a rationalization that was theologically suspect.

I hurried to the roast beef station. My mouth watered until it ached with gushing pangs as I watched the meat's juices ooze from the flesh and glisten down the breadth of the steamship round. The gardener in me recognized the presence of fragrant French thyme. I also detected a hint of chopped rosemary. Of course, there was garlic, too, and flat leaf parsley. I was glad to see that the ladle for jus was quite deep, and I was sure to request two dips, not one, and an extra dollop of the horseradish cream with freshly ground black pepper.

I looked over the carver's tattooed neck as he bobbed up and down with slicing motions, and I thought how perfectly the meat had been cooked to medium rare. My toothsome portion fell off the bone with an amenable drape that signaled the beef was yielding itself up for my enjoyment. The knifeman from Trinidad scooped a ladle of au jus and placed it on my plate with aplomb, almost as if he had grown the steer himself, his pride in it was so great. Our eyes met excitedly and he handed me my lunch with a little chuckle of indulgence at my gustatory anticipation.

What happened next can only mean that one of the mischievous fairies in the melons kicked a sizzling onion off of its skewer sword, and it rolled, still smoking with a lavender flame, onto the carpet that leads to the inner sanctum of my mind where my worst and darkest fears reside. That is to say, for some reason, the locus of my attention changed.

With my plate in my hand, I happened to glance into the window that revealed the interior of the kitchen. I suppose the window was meant to allow the guests to enjoy watching their meal preparation. Inside, a furious manager in spotless officer's whites forcefully shook his finger in front of an underling's face. A dressing down was taking place.

While I watched, a waiter toting water pitchers covered in humid pearls of condensation rushed recklessly through the kitchen's swinging doors, dropping a large linen napkin between them. It was caught in the threshold. The doors became stuck a foot short of fully closing. Through these open doors, I could clearly overhear the conversation echoing inside the stainless-steel enclave. My feet seemed cemented to the floor while I listened.

"Too much is from Bermuda left over," the food and beverage manager complained. He cast his critical Finnish gaze throughout the kitchen, encompassing the whole hot space. "Why so much food, Danilo? Did you on job drink again?"

The nervous Filipino chef removed his fluted hat and held it restlessly in his brown hands. "No, I did not drink. Please don't point at me like that."

"You Pinoy, when you point, you think it a ghost brings, yes?"

The chef put his hat back on. He knew that he was being insulted. He kept his temper in check nonetheless. "I will explain."

"Have you ever ghosts seen, Chef?" The manager toyed with Danilo.

The chef did not admit to believing the Filipino superstition. He replied calmly. "The European guests, they disliked the dry white wines, and we were overstocked. The Americans, they gobbled everything but the fish, which left us too much snapper." The chef knew that he would find no sympathy, but he continued. He took his time to formally add the b's and f's he usually deleted in his native Tagalog. "Then, after it rained, everybody went to the pool. No one came to the buffet."

"That is what you say," the manager rebuked. "Maybe ghost kept everyone away. A better plan from ghost would save all this waste, Danilo." The officer pointed haughtily around the kitchen. "I want this restaurant the Vasodilator Diet to serve by sundown, clear? You have provisions. This is special trip. Be ready!"

The chef nodded.

"And don't forget, I from the ceiling cameras watch. I see who eats. If they don't eat, you know what happens?"

"I know."

"It their blood affects. Culled they get. You want culled like them to be, Danilo?"

61

"No!" The chef held up his hand, waving it in a wide motion, as if cleaning off the refrigerator. "They will eat."

"Good! Put Bermuda food in incinerator. No need for now."

The officer exited through the swinging doors, kicking the napkin aside.

I felt my knees weaken. My wrists wilted like sun-struck flowers, and I lost control of my hands. I dropped my china dinner plate. It shattered across my feet, breaking into a thousand shards and making a dreadful noise. My eyes looked down to my shoes as if from a great, impassable distance away, watching the jus separate into oily rivulets over the polished leather. A quote from the book of Job came into my mind, unbidden: "Behold, you have instructed many, and you have strengthened the weak hands. Your words have upheld him who was stumbling, and you have made firm the feeble knees." If only, for me.

I could not deny any longer that everyone aboard the *Grand Rapina* except for Candace and myself knew precisely what this cruise was about. The ship was going to Latin America to take prisoners for a human blood experiment. They were all in on it, from the highest officer to the lowest cleaner, whether of their own volition or through some kind of coercion, and the facts had been concealed from my wife and me. Had we been chosen for the depth of our naiveté? Had we been considered patsies and easy marks? What was our role to be, and when was it to be explained to us?

Candace led me to the nearest table to sit down. She pulled out a chair and helped me collapse into it. Kneeling, she held my hand. "Honey, can you hear me?" she whispered. Candace then called out in the empty dining room, hoping her voice would carry. "Somebody help me get my husband to the doctor!" my wife begged, looking around. "We need help!"

With my head between my hands, I crumbled at what I'd overheard, the plan for a diet to impact everybody's blood, for purposes bound to be bad. Related hints at the madness flooded my mind. I remembered the old man at the dock who'd been corralled back into the ship like an animal. I remembered the cryptic officer in the atrium, with his pronouncements about rough sailing and sarcasm about God's protection, and his ridicule of me on the ship's bridge. I wasn't welcome there because pawns are never the villains' equals. How they must have joked about me when I'd fled! To them I was just a stupid, silly old man, chosen for his stupid, gullible pride, someone to be manipulated like a hollow puppet on a string.

In my mind, I could still see the bloody syringe and dripping gauze in the planter, and the spiny lizard that had scaled the foliage and then my imagination. Someone was practicing, it would seem, and he was so appallingly bold and unrepentant that he did not even care to conceal his murderous intentions. I recalled the funereal drapes over the blinded slot machines, the darkened display cases in the jewelry store, and the vacant dance floor crippled with stillness. The victims would not be needing these, so why bother to open them? All of the evidence for impending horror was around me in plain sight. No wonder I'd had a sense of foreboding. The *Grand Rapina* effused a misuse of everything's natural purpose and liveliness. Was I destined to be misused as well?

I absolutely did not know what to do. I had no resources of experience to deal with this crisis. I could only plead to God in a stunned and quivering posture. I realized that I was about to be an unwilling party to something despicable on the high seas. I was trapped!

My heart sank into inexpressible heaviness. I found that my spirit returned to memories of home. I longed for the tranquility of my flower garden, whose soft scents had always calmed me in years past. I tried to block out the ship. I knew that on Carlton Street, it was time to mow the grass. The bird bath would need refilling. The tool shed would need fresh paint, and the shovels would have to be sharpened before storing them for the winter. I wanted to go home, right away, and with Candy, and if we ever returned there, I would never think about leaving again. I'd owned an acre of heaven, and I had thrown it away!

It was at this moment that the candle of optimism that had thus far illuminated my life went dark. This light was extinguished in me as if it had been snuffed out in a nor'easter of panic. I descended into a pessimism that was nearly paralyzing as I faced the reality that the *Grand Rapina* was a watery, violent prison on the order of Mamertine in Rome, where Peter and Paul had been held in chains in the massive cistern. I could scarcely breathe, even. God had allowed to expire in me a hopeful, carefree temperament, which was replaced with a prisoner of war's trembling terror. The friendly, malleable core of my being began to harden into the iron point on an arrow, which I knew I would have to learn to aim with deadly skill to live.

In my weakness, hindered by confusion, I mumbled incoherent fragments to Candy. "This ship, this cruise. Something's wrong." I burst into tears. I was overcome by an awareness of evil that I couldn't push down. Looking back, I might have just moaned.

My wonderful, vivacious wife, my wise companion of nearly forty years, stayed down on her arthritic knees to listen. She seemed relieved as I babbled. "I know. Honey, I know. I feel it, too." My spouse blotted my tears with the hem of her tunic.

"I'm sorry I brought you here, Candy. I'm so sorry. I wanted to keep it from you and keep you safe."

"What's the matter? What do you mean? What are you hiding?"

"They're going to take blood. They're going to feed them and then take their blood."

"Whose blood?"

"The people who get on board."

Candace turned white as a sheet. "How do you know that?"

"I heard them talking about it in the kitchen."

The carver from the buffet suddenly walked toward me with a folded wheelchair. He'd pulled it from a corner somewhere, and he proceeded to lift me into it gingerly.

"Come on, Mista' Reverend, we goin' down to da' medical centa'. You just hold on. It goin' be all right." The worker pushed me briskly toward the elevator, with Candace following.

When we'd descended down eight stories and the doors opened into a broad hallway, the carver from Trinidad pushed me a short distance to the infirmary. "I've got him from here," Candy said. "I appreciate your help." She patted my shoulder and took over the driving. The carver returned to the elevator.

My wife pushed me into a bay of cubicles, each separated by a long curtain on rings and containing a hospital bed. The lights in the space were faintly yellow and painfully harsh. An antiseptic smell permeated the floors and the walls. I've always hated the smell of peroxide. As I tried to rise up and exit the wheelchair, I reached out for something to grasp, a table's edge or a bedside chair.

I heard my wife, behind me, step aside and then stop.

I hung my hand over the wheelchair without turning around, knowing with confidence that Candace would take it and steady me. Her grip was strong and sure, as usual. When I was able to finally stand up, I turned to thank my darling wife and looked straight into the calculating eyes of Doctor Jenny Elihu, the ship's physician.

"Well, we meet again," Jenny said. She let go of my hand. "I understand you're having a dizzy spell. Sit back down, please."

I didn't reply and only stared at Jenny angrily. She had to know about the *Grand Rapina*'s mission. She might have even designed it.

"You should be more careful when you eavesdrop," the doctor ridiculed.

"How did you know I overheard? Did the Finnish elk god call you?"

"Who, Alvar Hanka? No, no. Chef Danilo sent me a text."

Jenny ran her stethoscope over my chest. Then she waved a small flashlight off and on in front of both of my eyes. I wondered if she could see my hatred for her gazing back.

"They were talking openly about culling people."

"Danilo's just on edge. He drinks too much. He's afraid he's going to get put off the ship in Fort Lauderdale, with no money home to the Philippines."

"He's afraid of more than that."

"Follow my finger and look this way, to the right," Jenny said. "That's good. Now, follow my finger and look to the left. Have you had plenty of water today? Give me your arm. I want to take your blood pressure." She pulled the long band from her white jacket.

"Don't play games with me, Jenny. I know what this cruise is about."

Jenny was unruffled. "You do? And what is this cruise really about?"

"You're going to experiment on people!" Candy shouted.

Jenny moved her gaze from me to my wife. "Mrs. Atterley, are you feeling sick, too?"

"I feel fine and I've never been more clear-headed!"

"I'm not so sure. You seem feverish to me. I think I'll have both of you stay in your cabin for a few days. We'll send you your meals and everything you need." Jenny looked at Candace and me condescendingly. "We have to make sure you don't spread any virus."

Two heavyset orderlies appeared from behind the cubicle's curtain with a second wheelchair. They were emotionless and in the doctor's thrall.

Jenny looked at the men officiously and gave her orders. "Take the pastor and his wife to their stateroom and keep them there. A brief quarantine is needed." To Candy and me, Jenny announced our total dependence on her. "I'll tell you when you're feeling better," the doctor said. "I'll know you're recovered when you're talking sense again." Jenny pulled the curtain aside to leave us. "You might want to think about how much you'd like to see the sights. It would be a shame if you were confined for the whole trip."

"Get away from us," I seethed. "You're going to burn for this."

"And once in a while, it's a shame, but some people never recover from your ailment. Keep that in mind."

Candy and I glanced at one another as Jenny's threat hung in the air.

For the first time in our lives, my wife and I were deprived of our freedom.

CHAPTER FIVE

About seventy-five miles out of Charleston, the *Grand Rapina* hit the Gulf Stream and she rolled for hours, almost making me glad that I was trapped in my room, in my bed. I could not believe that such a state-of-the-art ship would so disturbingly rock in the warm, rushing currents. Having never been on the high seas before, though a native South Carolinian, I had no idea that I was prone to violent sea sickness. I refused to beg Jenny Elihu for motion sickness pills. In contrast to me, Candace seemed as placid as a snail. Her steadiness filled me with envy. My wife took to the ocean waters immediately, if not to our actual captivity in our stateroom. Inside it, she paced.

It has been written that Ponce de Leon discovered the Gulf Stream, and Benjamin Franklin was one of the first to chart it, from its origins off of Africa, around the Gulf of Mexico, through the Florida Straits, up the east coasts of the United States and Canada, and then over to Europe in what is known as the Northern Drift. Personally, I think they can keep it all. It made me miserable. Two days after leaving Charleston, I was still mainly sleeping as we passed right on by Port Everglades in Florida, the Captain apparently believing we needed nothing and not wanting to attract attention.

Later, while briefly docked in Key West, the steward Chris Adamos entered our room and locked our balcony doors, I suppose thinking we would stand on our terrace and shout for help. I did get a glimpse of the yachts that dock in Key West from all over the world, and, judging from the way they bobbed in the water, I noticed that the wind had picked up precipitously. If only the *Grand Rapina* would have smashed into her berth in the crosswinds, but she did not.

I finally developed some sea legs in the Gulf of Mexico. There, the Captain sent us a note, how gracious of him! He said we would make for

Cozumel, in the Caribbean. I understood that to mean he would now need me to "chaplain" the new "guests." Since everything that the Captain did surprised me, I was confused when he announced over the intercom that we would drop anchor offshore. Looking back, I think that he did not want his ship inspected.

By Latin American standards, the people of the resort area known as Cozumel, Mexico, are prosperous, at least in the quarters near the cruise ship terminal. There, most of the citizens are sustained by tourists, unlike those on the more rural side of the island. The lifestyles in Cozumel are not American, nor should they be. By comparison, it is easy to erroneously consider them inferior. As I learned more about the people of Cozumel, I came to increasingly value their culture.

When night came, and after Candace and I had been fed like pets by the steward, I was startled to hear the rumble of small boats. I heard voices, too, some excited, all of them in Spanish. What I was hearing was the tendering of people out of the port to the *Grand Rapina*, which necessitated a wide assortment of bribes for local officials, I'm sure. This flow of onboarding lasted for over an hour and then was suddenly silent. Somewhere, these unfortunates were being hidden away and doubtless being told that they were on their way to a bright future in America. I shudder to think of it.

When dawn arrived, I had already spent hours reading my Bible. Breakfast was cold and bland, yet the steward unlocked the doors to our balcony, not out of any kind of mercy, but because he knew that we were too far away from the shoreline to signal for assistance. The sunlight felt so wonderful on my skin as the sun rose higher, and reading the Gospel in the natural light invigorated me. If we had not been prisoners, Candy and I would have enjoyed even our meal of meager soggy oatmeal out on the terrace.

What had made those in Cozumel flock to the *Grand Rapina*? I did not know, at that moment, but I knew for certain what had been asked of them: Give us a single drop of your blood, and come away to a new world. Only a few hours after the refugees' onboarding, I was summoned to the Starlight Deck, which contained the ship's spa and the pool that had enticed away all of Chef Danilo's diners. I was to discover that, incredibly, almost all of those who had been transported to the ship from Cozumel were women from poor regions.

In upcoming days, I was stupefied to learn from them as their new chaplain that although they were nominally Christian, mainly Catholic, most of them were familiar practitioners of ancient Mayan rituals performed for hundreds of years on the island of Cozumel, including the female rituals of donating their monthly menstrual flow to a goddess, to ensure fertility or in gratitude for it.

So these women were accustomed to the idea of giving up their blood, and some thought that they, indeed, had the best part of the bargain on the *Grand Rapina* voyage. Who would not want to go to America? The women thought that giving a little blood on a comfortable ocean liner in exchange for a "better" life was no obstacle at all, a small price to pay, especially considering that the women were descended from hardy Mayan forebears who had literally walked from all over Central America to come to Cozumel to offer their femininity in the divine temples.

Whoever had designed the "Blood for Sail" cruise, with its sinister appeal, knew of these women's religious background, this population's vulnerability, and had targeted them for exploitation with a customized message about offering their blood. Someone had looked into their history, and how best to reach them, emotionally. The women's simple trust in a promise from what must have been, to them, a reputable source aroused in me simultaneously pity and outrage.

I walked the Starlight Deck as one about to go to a funeral. The women, however, were quietly jubilant. A little girl about ten years of age named Emmanuella spontaneously translated for me, and she was so excited about being promised a bath in the spa by the crew who had brought her aboard. "They're going to bathe me with rose petals and let me swim in the pool!" she declared in the perfect English she'd learned in a new public school, an asset her bricklayer father had never enjoyed from a Mexican government lately motivated to improve student fluency for economic expansion. Where was Emmanuella's father? Was her mother onboard? Apparently, the little girl's family believed she would be better off in the States; hence her presence on the ship.

My heart ached at the girl's misplaced faith in the *Grand Rapina*'s crew. She was the tiniest of prey for them. While still trying to gauge the situation, I was brusquely escorted back to my stateroom by Chris Adamos. There, I had my own mattress and a bathroom. The women from Cozumel were being bedded down directly on the floor as I was ushered out. How they would be cared for I had no idea, and how ironically macabre it had been to tempt them with spa treatments. This trip would be so far away from a luxurious adventure for the Cozumel women that they'd be lucky to survive it.

It is rare as a pastor that I am taken aback, but the women's personal stories, with their hopeful yearnings for a happy family life in the States, and their undampened national pride even in the face of fleeing Mexico, and their syncretistic spiritual faith, put me off balance. It was all exotic to me. We had our humanity in common, that's true, and presumably the Christian religion, but when I looked into their faces, so unlike my own, I felt that we were the most distant of relatives, and certainly not cousins. In time, this feeling of odd unfamiliarity wore off and was replaced with a sense of solid kinship.

But upon meeting the women, I gave them all a blessing and said little else, for the time being. I had so much "Otherness" to think about, other races and other gods. Through these Cozumel women, I was confronted with the God of the Bible and with something else, something potentially vicious, something that sent babies to desperate wives (or so they thought), and then demanded them back in horrific human sacrifice, at least in ancient times. This "divine" intercessor was a person who was real to them, a benevolent goddess one day and a fiend the next, someone who was simply one of several supernatural beings, including Christ, who must be begged and placated.

In my understanding, I knew this creature by a different name, and knew him to be the fallen one, the Lord's enemy. He was part of the deception that had drawn the Cozumel women to the *Grand Rapina*. I was not sure that I was the right pastor to try to tease out pagan traditions from Christian theology, but I was the only clergy on the boat, so there you have it. Unlike previous times in my life, when I was able to refrain from saying everything that I thought I knew to maintain decorum, in this situation, on the contrary, I would have to share everything that I deeply believed in order to help those in danger.

This initial encounter on the grotesquely misnamed "Starlight Deck," which proved to be the darkest launching pad for a great evil, was only the first of many times that I would contemplate my own Christian beliefs on the terrible *Grand Rapina*. Helping the Cozumel women, and those who came later from other countries, became my life's mission.

I hope that my trial judges will believe me, for I am also, in the end, a person who must depend, in faith, on trustworthy authorities. Lord, let me not be disappointed.

The *Grand Rapina* sailed on to Belize. Soon, I heard tender boats in the darkness again, this time as the wicked ocean liner dropped anchor in the shallow Caribbean waters that were home to the favorite coral reef of Charles Darwin. Captain Moze Balodis was despicable, but as a sailor, he knew enough to stay a couple of miles offshore to avoid running his ship aground on the reef, a catastrophe that I would've enjoyed very much, especially since I had discovered from hours of watching closed circuit television that an American embassy was only about forty miles away from the port in Belize City. I would have been willing to jump overboard and bloody my feet to shreds on the sharp, spiraling coral to swim straight to my compatriots in the embassy, if I had been younger.

Around midnight, since our balcony doors were open, I stepped out onto our terrace to see what I could of the runaways boarding our vessel. The moonlight was intense. This time, the melee included both men and women. I believe that I heard voices in Spanish and quite a few in English. As only an amateur linguist, I also thought for all the world that I was hearing "Creole," which later proved to be barely translatable for little Emmie, who was glad when the new refugees switched back to their common currency of Spanish. Why had they come? What had driven these people in Belize to make an escape on the ocean?

The next morning, when I was called to minister to these most recent refugees, I was struck by two things: First, and I suppose that this was anthropology in action, I saw that the Cozumel women and children had begun to purposely separate themselves from the newly arrived Belizeans. This was fine with the runaways from Belize, and although they had arrived second on the ship and lost out on claiming the most comfortable, padded floorboards on the Starlight Deck, they began to form their own separate territory by communicating in their native Kriol, thus excluding the Cozumel group from understanding them. And since they couldn't have the nicest floors, they chose to be near the nicest windows. The Belizeans made their own enclave, based on their language. It disheartened me that seemingly no matter the desperate situation, human beings will always sort themselves in this way.

The second thing that struck me was that I was immediately mistaken for a priest. This confusion was bound to happen, and I went so far as to consider removing my collar to avoid it. I feared, however, that if I did, I would lose my legitimacy among the people as their chaplain, so I left it on. With the symbolism of my collar for all to see, I discovered that there was among many an urgency for me to hear their confessions.

To the first few refugees, in full disclosure I advised that I was Protestant, not Catholic, but in a few minutes, it did not seem to matter. They assumed that I was the man that God had placed on the *Grand Rapina* for them, and that was enough. They did not realize that I was a prisoner, and I did not think it wise just yet to confide in the refugees. Looking back, I think that my pastoral instincts discounted my own captivity to minister to the runaways.

Out of their confessions came the people's heartbreaking reasons for fleeing Belize. These they delivered in English, mainly, while Emmie stood reverently behind me to translate the occasional Spanish phrase. She and I, working together, usually deduced the patois Kriol, too. There were sins recounted with profound contrition by some, who even worried that I might refuse to absolve them, and sins noted with casual, perfunctory obligation by others. I noticed that often those with the most "minor" sins wept with the most regret, while those with the most "serious" sins revealed them to me to receive forgiveness as from a robot programmed to automatically relay it.

I struggled with allowing Emmie to serve as my translator, for she was only a child, and I did not want to expose her to the blatant violations of the Ten Commandments that I heard, nor generally to the manifold, pitiful traumas expressed. I regret that working with Emmie was just one of the many unethical things — in common parlance, professional infractions — that I myself committed on the *Grand Rapina*. Left and right on this voyage, I had to do things that I would not have done, ordinarily. Some allowances should be made for my circumstances, shouldn't they? It is not true that I committed crimes, though! My actions were always justified, considering. I want my trial judges to know that.

At the bottom of most of the runaways' agonies, one way or another, was usually extreme, unrelenting poverty. People steal in order to eat when they're poor; they lie and connive when they are without hope for a better economic future. Some people become nihilistic, others physically cruel. And those who might do their best to alter their disadvantaged destiny often rebel with bad outcomes when they are despised by outsiders and blamed for their lot, when they are guilty of little more than being born.

And, yes, admittedly, some people do willfully, exuberantly sin, because for a while it is fun and feels good, or is expedient, or self-promoting, or apparently without consequences, or for more reasons why than the greatest theologians have ever imagined. Even the holy angels refrain from guessing why. Only God understands the renegade hearts, and I never trust myself to apply labels to them. I am not in the condemnation business.

Poverty diminishes the Belizean people's gifts, and it drove scores to the *Grand Rapina*, dragging what was left of their innocence after them. Who was I to be their confessor? Well, I was the only one around remotely qualified. I, myself, reluctantly concluded that I was the man the Lord had installed for the purpose. I felt I had to stand in the breach. In the pressure of having to act, I had to decide that I was not onboard by accident.

Our death cruise continued. We made for Roatan Port, in the Bay Islands, off the northern coast of Honduras. I know this because Captain Balodis sent Chris Adamos on a special errand to tell me to stay in my quarters, even to keep off of the balcony, because of the danger. For his own horrid purposes, and in a twist on Stockholm Syndrome, the Captain intended to keep me safe with a personalized "head's up." In my mind, I set fence posts and barbed wire around any gesture of helpfulness from the man who was steering a rogue ocean liner en route to imprisoning people. He was not to be seen as endearing.

Chris Adamos cared so very much about my welfare. "If you escape off this ship in Honduras, you're dead," he warned. I realized then that we'd have to dock in the port, making a run to land possible. The steward wagged a finger at me like a parent. "These people have nothing better to do than invent crazy new ways to torture you, and they're very creative. The violence is incredible. Don't risk it!" How nice of my captor to try to protect me, while the psychological warfare continued. I think that Captain Balodis just wanted to save me for the joy of killing me later, himself.

"And by the way," Chris continued approvingly. "The guests are calm and quiet. Whatever it is you're doing, keep it up. The Captain says you're doing a good job." I see now. I had the Devil's dubious endorsement. Believing me sufficiently cowed by his terror-inducing warnings, the steward did not bother to lock our balcony doors before he left.

We approached Roatan Port in full daylight. Of course, Candy and I went out on our balcony, anyway, to watch. I am not about to take orders from thugs. As we neared the cruise ship dock, we saw acres of white sandy beaches on one side, with groups of snorkelers entering the cerulean water as they walked out from a jungle of swaying palm trees. As with so many ports in the Caribbean, the wind was brisk, making the waves foam. On the other side of our terrace, to the north, we saw a shopping complex, rather shabby but undergoing renovation, with a large, incongruous sign that was hawking good prices on diamond jewelry. The closer we got to shore, the more I could smell some sort of deep frying of fruit, probably plantains.

Government corruption runs so deep there, and crime is so obviously rampant, that the Hondurans who wanted to flee simply stood in line at the dock, in the open. There was no need to pretend. The refugees had paid the necessary bribes, scraping the funds together from family members who hoped to soon follow to the States, and the local officials had pocketed the money and literally opened the gates that surrounded the mall area where the port is. No pretenses or disguises were involved, although I suppose that if a famous magazine had been on site taking photos, all of the Hondurans would've claimed to be taking new jobs on the *Grand Rapina*. But the fact is that they were running for their lives, which they planned to save, paradoxically, by giving of their lifeblood.

The ocean liner floated safely into port. Candy and I retreated into our cabin to wait for me to be called to meet the newest "guests." As I was drawing our curtains to block the dazzling tropical sun, gunshots rang out. The crowd below scrambled and screamed. I stepped quickly back onto the balcony.

On the dock below, a few rumpled policemen gathered. The crowd parted to let them through to a young man who had been attacked while standing in line. Whoever had shot the boy had simply wandered away, not even pursued by the law enforcement that saw a murder in broad daylight as just another day in the office. Not one of the officers appeared to be in a rush to follow the perpetrator, and I would swear that one of them stood idly around slowly eating a hand pie.

A crew member yelled from one of the lower decks. "What happened? Do you need any help?"

The police casually asked a question or two of the crowd and then responded in broken English. "He cut the line. Somebody got mad. Now, he's no more a problem."

"That's not true!" a young woman sobbed. Her brown eyes were wide with anger. She must have been the boy's sister. "Marco was waiting with me! They killed him to steal his phone!"

No ambulance came because nobody cared. If he had been taken to a hospital, the young man would have been ignored in favor of patching up the wounds of the local cartel leaders, who commandeered the doctors' attention and most of the medications as well. If Marco had received any attention at all, it would have been from the missionaries, who cared for the sick and fed the gaunt prisoners in the nearby jail in their damp, claustrophobic cells.

As it was, a stretcher was brought from the jail, and Marco's ravaged body was lifted onto it by the policemen. The one in charge spoke officiously to an underling. "You don't get that blood on me!" Someone led the crying sister away, taking her by the arm and out of the crowd, which immediately reassembled and readied to board the *Grand Rapina* as if nothing had happened. In a short while, there was excited laughter. Unbelievable.

When I was summoned to be the chaplain to this group, I thought hard about refusing. "What did I tell you? I told you so!" Chris Adamos admonished.

I prayed to recover my compassion for the Hondurans, and to see them as children of God. I worried that the murderer was still among those boarding the ship, and that he would wreak havoc in the dark confines of the Starlight Deck.

The next day, and not a moment too soon, we set out for the Port of Limon in Costa Rica.

Not long after, I was unexpectedly delighted as a sweet breeze filled our cabin. Candace noticed it, too. The aroma evoked memories of doughnut shops and bakeries. As I walked out on the balcony to investigate the source of the smell, I was surprised to see on the horizon a multitude of burly cargo ships, each laden with tons of coffee and bananas. I'm no gourmet, but I thought that the smell emitting from those ships was close to but not exactly like what I was experiencing. As we drew near to the dock, which was in terrible shape and nearly falling down in its rusting deterioration, I had the first long laugh that I'd had for days. As the *Grand Rapina* made her way to the cruise ship pier, I actually chortled aloud.

It was pineapples! I was smelling fresh pineapples! They were being loaded for export. I instantly thought of all the upside-down cakes I'd eaten in South Carolina, often baked into caramel gooiness by parishioners in gratitude for a lovely christening service. How strange it was to smell this happy scent from home! The warm feeling wasn't to last too long, though.

We sat in Limon for a day, and, from what I could see, no refugees came near the *Grand Rapina.* I saw being loaded only a few Masterson crates full of avocadoes and guavas, probably requested by Chef Danilo to prevent scurvy in the "guests." There was virtually no foot traffic, none of the crowds that before had been eager to enter the ship. Candace was suffering with a migraine again from the stress of this voyage, and for that reason I decided not to make a break for it onto the dock. I could never leave Candy behind, even to run for help, for retaliation on my wife would have been swift and heartless.

So I watched the cargo ships for a while and then came indoors to plot how I might escape from within. Would it be possible to penetrate the cabin's ceiling and escape through the ductwork? What if I set our room on fire, to attract attention from the port officials? No, I decided against it, fearing that Captain Balodis would simply let us burn up. I checked on Candace. She was in some pain.

Chris Adamos came with food at dinnertime. He was distracted. I noticed that he was wearing a thick gold, Cuban link chain over his uniform shirt. He'd come into some money, apparently. He seemed like the kind of warped soul who would decide this was the right time to display it.

"Why are we in this port? No one seems to have boarded."

"That's right. No new guests today."

"Then why are we here?"

"Limon is close to the Panama Canal. We're going through, over to the Pacific side of Central America and on down to the South."

This was a treasure trove of information from my captor, unless he was lying.

"Get ready to preach again in the morning. I'll come as usual," the steward said.

On the Starlight Deck the next day, I walked as calmly as I could among the refugees. I was greeted by many now-familiar faces. At least everyone looked as if they were being fed. Curiously, Emmie did not come to say good morning, and I soon saw that she was in deep conversation with a young girl sitting morosely in a corner. I'd never seen this child before. The girl was accompanied by a sullen older man who was vigorously engaged in shooing Emmanuella away. "Get lost, she's none of your business!" I heard him scolding. My Spanish was improving, by necessity.

I walked over to defend my young translator. What I saw shook me so deeply in a horrific revelation that I was nearly physically ill. In the great crime of imminent bloodletting that I knew was about to take place against the runaways, another crime was occurring. My naiveté shattered at the sight of a crime within a crime. I was seeing Costa Rica's great plague: human trafficking.

The little girl lifted her sleepy, dark eyes to look at me and then rolled them away, exhausted. She was about eleven years old, a pre-teen. Her emerging puberty was barely covered in a scant tube top and shorts. "Daddy," she said weakly, "who is that?" If I never say another sentence in my remaining years, let me now proclaim in all outrage that this child of the living God was tattooed on the right side of her delicate neck with a pink rose above a black crown. When she turned to speak to her male companion, I saw on her left side the devastating mark of a dollar sign also etched into her skin. I knew from my previous pastoral training in child abuse prevention that this little one was for sale.

So, we had no new "guests" yesterday on the *Grand Rapina*?

Trying to understand a criminal's lawless mind, I realized that Chris Adamos had spirited this child and her captor onboard, both unseen, and that he had been rewarded with a new chain necklace made from gold. What else had been smuggled onto the *Grand Rapina*? Captain Balodis wasn't going to park a cruise liner so that a steward could have a new trinket.

The girl's keeper looked up at me in seething defiance. He was reeking and agitated. His unrestrained depravity had no shame, and he sat in his corner guarding his property like a mad dog.

I moved Emmie away. I had to think.

The Starlight Deck was so heavy with evil that I thought it might sink the ship.

I had to depend on God like never before in my life. Would he be there for me on the Pacific side of the Panama Canal?

* * *

The man with the smooth, white skin returned his fork to its place on the soft linen. An investment banker in New York, he insisted that everything remain in its proper place, including his staff. At dinner this day, inside a gold-monogrammed border etched deeply onto his china plate, a Wagyu rib eye steak lay, overcooked. The food had been placed at his table while he had made his way to it in his private elevator. The meat lay like the blackened, upturned palm of a hand, severely, even spitefully, burned.

The banker adjusted his Italian wool cuffs. He pushed a small red button that was kept beside his crystal water glass at every meal. For years, he had pushed this button briefly, lightly, to receive an instantaneous response from the servant on the other end, for that was the button's function: to make known his every desire. The banker had purchased the deluxe button model, and had had it shipped to him via his own international shipping company, Masterson Maritime. According to every expert, it was the very best button.

This button now buzzed according to its design to do its owner's bidding. The banker expected the same of the insolent cook, the man who had doomed himself by serving wrecked beef. Anything less than perfection — measured by his own mercurial definition — the banker took as a personal affront, especially when it involved one of his appetites. The man pressed the red button again, and again, and held it down to listen to its loud urgency.

"Yes, Mr. Masterson?" a voice responded from out of the speaker where the button rested. It was an inappropriately neutral voice, the banker believed. It did not grieve at its offense. It did not sound hurried to make amends. The tone was unacceptable.

"Come at once." The banker stiffened his back. The salt shaker toppled.

A uniformed cook entered the heavily brocaded dining room, but just barely, as he leaned against the door. His sweat left a mark on the raised panels. The servant seemed to be avoiding a force field that invisibly surrounded the banker. The cook would not come close. He kept his distance. "What do you need, Mr. Masterson? What can I bring you?"

Dominating the pause, the banker took a long moment to gaze out of the Palladian window and into his manicured garden. He noticed that the peonies were dripping nectar on the other side of the glass, and ants gathered. As if he could eradicate the insects from a distance, destroy them with his sheer will, the banker spread open his fingers on the tablecloth and imperceptibly crushed the four-leaf-clover pattern woven by Irish nuns. In his mind's eye, Mr. Masterson wiped away the offending, inconsequential ants. "John, I must tell you that I am shocked by your behavior."

The cook said nothing. His heart began to pound.

Mr. Masterson took his checkbook, which was always on his person, out of his jacket pocket. He opened it slowly, thumbed a few pages, and laid it flat on the luxurious tablecloth, pushing his plate aside with disgust and blowing out the candelabra, too. The banker also brought forth a gold pen, old school and heavy, and placed it very deliberately on top of the paper checks. Clearly, he was preparing for something.

The cook gripped the doorknob behind him.

The banker suddenly whirled to confront the servant. "You know I want to see blood!" he screamed. "How dare you bring me this garbage!"

For what was about to take place, the cook did not blame the grocer or the butler. It was now or never. He took a step forward and willingly pushed his career off of a cliff. "You always want blood from some poor creature, first the steak's, then mine! I'm not going to bleed for you anymore!"

"You will do what I want with what I pay for! Apologize!"

"That's not going to happen!"

"You're nothing, just a piece of shit!"

"I should poison you!"

The banker's face turned white and crimson in apoplectic anger. His full lips trembled. In a rage, he scrawled a check and flung it at the impertinent cook. "Get out," Mr. Masterson commanded menacingly. "Get out of my house now, or I will string you up and pour gasoline on you!"

"You'll do *what?*" the cook reflexively laughed. He grabbed the check from where it had fluttered down on the floor, and then fled. "You're *crazy*, you bat shit old man!"

Of course, the ants continued to gather.

CHAPTER SIX

In Panama, at the Port of Colon, they came to the *Grand Rapina* as if drawn by a malevolent Pied Piper. In a pouring rain, they came in jostling crowds, pushing up against the chain link fences that separated the dock from the crumbling tenements, where their ragged, soaked laundry was still pinned on lines strung between broken windows. Motorcycles and bikes had been abandoned in alleys as the refugees answered the piper's mysterious call, and cars with their engines still running had been discarded in the narrow streets. Though its origins were still unknown to me, the runaways understood the hidden signal to run, run for your life.

On that sweltering, tropical morning, when the heat rose from the seawater and the wet concrete buildings as if from a skillet, I prayed for the masses swirling toward the *Grand Rapina*. This crowd included not only Panamanian locals, but it appeared to contain many from across Latin America, judging from their faces' motley shades of brown and black. I assumed they were fleeing from their own troubled nations such as Columbia, having barely survived a trek through the ruthless Darien Gap, a snake-infested, cartel-oppressed jungle that is the only land bridge to connect South America to Central America. Once through this dangerous habitat and into Panama, the South American migrants would have moved north and then east to Colon, to combine with those native Panamanians who also hoped to make their way to the States via the *Grand Rapina*.

Were my prayers reaching heaven, or were they snagged in the humid clouds above or on the churning flesh below? Some of the runaways had brought squawking birds, and some carried half-starved dogs. I saw a monkey with a nearly human face jumping from shoulder

81

to shoulder. One man bore on his back a trunk crammed full of pink flamingoes and royal blue butterflies. One woman gripped her handmade basket to her chest, cherishing it and the live baby crocodile that it contained. The dark-haired children carried plump knit dolls. The white-haired elders, many of whom were from nearby indigenous tribes, came proud and empty-handed, wearing the neon geometric fabrics inspired by the ancient body painting that some of my conservative missionary colleagues so disapproved of.

They came willingly, earnestly, for they'd been promised a new and prosperous life. All they had to do was give up a drop of their blood, so they thought. A treacherous tale by Majestic Waves Cruise Lines had been passed secretly from countryside hut to countryside hut, throughout the villages and the jungles and the cities, and the people came in a hypnotic exodus of desperation. They had no idea that their lifeblood would become the currency for an evil taskmaster's fortunes, fortunes intended to wipe them off the earth.

While the rain slowly turned to steam, I looked out over the bay from my stateroom's balcony. This morning, we were the only cruise ship in the quay, but cargo ships were queued up in the distance, waiting for their turn to enter the canal locks en route to a full transit across to Fuerte Amador. I would have yelled for help for Candy and myself, but we were so high up on the *Grand Rapina* that no one would have heard us below, on streets noisy with screeching animals and screaming refugees.

As the eager runaways were rounded up by the ship's crew and guided into the lower decks, I knew that their poignant goals for a better life would never come to fruition, and I was hot and discouraged and weak in my own captivity. Sadly, I knew that in their own panicked dispersal, none of the refugees would have known how to help me and my wife, and it was too much to expect them to try.

Candy and I had been locked inside our cabin for days and days. I left our room only with an armed escort to calm the new arrivals. At the outset of this nightmarish cruise, our access to the ship's Wi-Fi had been disabled, and we were cut off from the world. We had only the maddening redundance of the same closed-circuit television programs that played over and over in an endless loop until I nearly memorized them, even with my aging faculties.

Though we had greater awareness about the *Grand Rapina* than the refugees, and were kept in more comfortable living conditions, Candy and I were likewise prisoners. We plotted to escape constantly. It became a game that we played, to remind ourselves that we might still exert control over our lives. Captain Balodis was not God. He could not confine us to hell forever. What if we tied all of our sheets, towels, drapes, and clothes together and attempted to scale the side of the ship, rappelling down one balcony at a time? I even thought of the hijinks of James Bond movies and MacGyver television shows, but no stunts came to mind that I was willing to try. Candace even thought of that old show "Bewitched," and how wonderful it would have been to simply wiggle our noses into freedom.

As I withdrew inside to our stateroom, too weary to watch the deluded parade in the rainy harbor of Colon any longer, I saw Candace scribbling on some stationery that she'd found in a dresser drawer. She was deep in thought, her brow furrowed. She didn't look up when I touched her on the back of her hair.

"Sweetheart, what are you doing?"

"I'm writing out my will."

I swallowed hard. "Please, Candy, no. We'll get through this."

"I had a dream. I think I'm supposed to write out my will."

I guessed that confinement was affecting my wife's emotions more than I knew. She began to describe what was more like an hallucination than even a nightmare. But who was I to judge? I was seeing flamingoes and butterflies and capuchin monkeys, myself. It was hard to keep track of what was real and what was not. Reality shimmered in the heat. Seclusion and stress were disorienting.

"I was wandering around our house, which was right on the edge of a large wood. I decided to go into our office to get some work done. I opened a big window, even though a plague was raging in the town, and lots of sunshine streamed in."

"All right, I can see you're going to tell me all about it. Go ahead." I sat down on the bed and unbuttoned my shirt. I had my own fears, but I had to listen to hers, too.

"I got lost in the work for a while, but then I looked up and saw that a beautiful, large wild owl had come into the office. It was perched across the room on the oak filing cabinet. It was a Great Horned Owl. It sat looking around, with large amber eyes and lots of feathers. It didn't make any sound, didn't poop or hoot or do anything. It just sat there, looking at me and around at the room.

"I opened the window wider, but the owl didn't fly out. I figured it would leave sometime during the day, and I went back to work. I was writing out my personal will, because there was a plague.

"At the end of the day, the owl was still sitting on the filing cabinet. I didn't know what to do with it. I closed the window enough to still give it room to fly out, then I closed the door to the office, and decided to go to bed. The owl would fly away on its own, I thought, during the night. It was a warm summer night. I could hear the forest sounds, especially the shrieking of rabbits being killed by foxes.

"The next morning, I was curious about the bird, and I still needed to work, so I went again into the office. To my surprise, the large owl had left, but it had been replaced by two smaller, fluffier owls. These came to me, were very friendly. I fluffed them up and played with them, like kittens. Then, they also perched on the filing cabinet and just hung around. They were also silent. No hooting.

"I left the window open that night again, but these birds, also, never left. I started getting used to the idea of living with owls. I decided if I was going to be an owl owner, I should probably figure out what to feed them. The office where I was working was a mess, but I foraged through some of the papers on the floor and the desk top, and didn't find any candy or anything edible, so I decided to go to the fridge for lunchmeat.

"I came back with the lunchmeat, and one of the birds came to me right away. The meat very much excited both birds, and I fed by hand the one that had flown to me. He gripped my fingers very hard with his talons, and as he ate, I could feel that his raptor beak was very sharp as he took the meat out of my fingers. I thought that this bird, really both birds, could've attacked me if they had wanted to, but for some reason they didn't.

"I lived with the birds for some weeks. They didn't make a mess, they didn't fly out the window, they didn't hoot, they were just there. I thought about ordering a cage for them online, but it really didn't seem to be needed. They never went anywhere.

"The plague escalated on and on.

"One day, I went into the office to work and see the birds, and I noticed that the feet of one of the birds had changed. They had gone from having dangerous claws to delicate, pink toes, like those of a mourning dove. That startled me, but it was strange for the owls to have come into my house in the first place, so I was sort of prepared for anything.

"In the next few days, the owl gradually morphed, from the bottom up. First, the talons changed, then the bottom shape of the bird changed, and then up to the whole body except for the head, and then one day I went inside the office, and there was one owl and one dove, both sitting on the filing cabinet.

"This struck me as an odd combination of companions. Couldn't the owl kill the dove? I left the window open for one of them to fly out.

"The next day, I went into the office and only the dove was there. The owl had flown out. The day after that, I went into the office and the dove had flown away, too. There were no birds living in my house any longer.

"I shut the window and locked it this time.

"I heard on the radio that the plague was over.

"And that was the end of my dream."

I sat with my head hanging down. Was Candy losing her mind? Was I? Bird invasions were happening right next to me, all night long in my bed, and I knew nothing about them. What else was going on that I didn't know about? What was I supposed to say regarding the phantasms that visited my ordinarily sensible wife? I had no idea how to interpret her visions. I lacked the seer Daniel's insight. Was Candy somehow influenced by leftover magic from the Festival of Diablos and Congos, a bacchanal during which the locals commemorated the slave rebellion that had overthrown their old Spanish masters? In Colon, they'd celebrated wildly in March. I'd read about such things on my postcards. Was there an occult power in the air, wafting up into the *Grand Rapina*?

Candy looked at me quizzically, seeking my opinion. "What do you suppose owls symbolize? And then there's the dove."

As I tried to think of something to say, I saw the tips of three fingers pushing a note under our cabin's door. The fingers put me in mind of the story of the ethereal hand that wrote on the wall in the royal Babylonian court, bringing a cryptic message of doom for King Belshazzar.

I picked up the note with my stomach in a knot. I prayed that it was a profuse apology for the way that we'd been treated from the corporate offices at Majestic Waves Cruises, as well as a plan for our disembarking in Colon, complete with free, first-class airfare back to South Carolina. One can hope! Instead, it was an invitation from Captain Moze Balodis to join him that night for dinner. "We've been summoned to have dinner with Rasputin." I ripped the invitation to pieces and flung them into the trash. "I'd rather starve."

"We have to eat," Candy replied, "even if it's with a monster."

At 6:00 p.m., the food that had been brought to our cabin regularly every evening ceased to come, but Chris Adamos came, in his formal dress uniform. He had no worries of Candy and me over-powering him in the hallway, I suppose. I was too old to try, and even if I had knocked him into unconsciousness with Candy's help, she and I would have been able to get no farther than to the end of the corridor, which was locked down, too.

"It's good to see you, Mrs. Atterley," the steward sneered.

"You won't get away with this, Chris. Somebody will find out, and you're all going to pay."

Chris's lip curled. "This way to the Captain's table. He's waiting for you."

As my first act of deliberate resistance, I wore an old white tee shirt, my blue jeans, and a pair of anklet socks in sneakers to dine with the Captain. I did not intend to show Moze Balodis any respect. This might seem like a small effort, but I was new at being a rebel. I had spent my whole adult life scrupulously obeying the rules — God's laws and man's — and not observing dinner proprieties with an authority figure represented a big challenge to my law-abiding nature.

Candace took a different approach. For her part, she dressed to the hilt. My wife always had a mind of her own. She intended to carry herself with all of the dignity that she could muster, even to dine with a barbarian, and she used her wardrobe, middle-class though it was, to demonstrate her unyielding insistence that civilized ways would prevail over injustice. I can see my wife in my mind's eye now, moving about on the *Grand Rapina* like a queen.

Candy combed her thinning hair into an elegant upsweep, which she secured with a rhinestone comb. She adorned herself with the one pair of small diamond earrings that she possessed, a gift to her from me on our wedding anniversary. She perfumed her neck, dabbing the glass stopper onto every wrinkle and sunspot. She colored her lips in carnelian. Candace wore her best evening attire, a floor-length gown made of yellow summery lace finished off with a little jacket. She wore satin shoes trimmed with bows and carried a small purse with a gold clasp that she'd had dyed to match. My wife looked so regal and aristocratic. She could not have looked more haughtily pulled together if she had been enrobed in yards and yards of ermine. Her indomitable spirit animated her outfit.

There we were, each of us clothed in our respective interpretation of social agitation. At every opportunity, I attempted a holy, mutinous resistance, and encouraged that disobedience in my spouse. I hope that the judges at my maritime trial will understand that I resisted the *Grand Rapina*'s menacing evil as best I knew how. It was a David and Goliath situation.

This first try at overtly objecting to cruelty was the hardest, for I was breaking through so many of my previous mindsets, such as believing that most people are essentially good and that they will try to do the right thing. I had to get over that belief in the perverse *Grand Rapina* community, and yet not forget that God has the power to limit the wickedness that people can do. Frankly, I am still trying to reconcile these ideas. At my Glenville church, I had never made a political statement other than insisting in the newsletter that the budget for the new grand piano would not be exceeded under any circumstances. In matters of sacred music, I was content with either the classic hymns or the contemporary catalogue. I cooperated. I negotiated. I acquiesced. Some people would have even called me a follower, not a leader. I thought of myself as a peace maker.

By temperament, I was not an ardent activist or a hot-headed rabble rouser. In fact, I was prone to falling asleep during committee meetings. I daydreamed while the secretary read the minutes. I did not much care if the carpet in the sanctuary were red or blue, and I did not think it worth the aggravation to argue for the merits of hardwood floors, which would have provided a longer-term solution to wear-and-tear issues than any rug. At funeral luncheons, I was just as happy to eat a quiche as a casserole. When they wanted to set the thermostat at sixty-nine degrees, it was fine with me, though I sometimes had to put on a heavier sweater. I was willing to compromise. I tried very hard never to be offended.

In matters of social justice, such as women's roles in the Church, I followed the guidelines of my denomination, and kept my disagreements with those pronouncements to myself. Regarding rituals, I was pleased to give communion at the altar, or, if need be, in the pew, wearing my stole and robes or just my clerical collar and slacks, with grape juice or with wine, in a morning or an evening service. For decades, I tried to make my church a home for the believer and a welcoming respite for the seeker. Even outright atheists, if I could ever attract them to attending one of my sermons, I never scorned with talk of a flaming afterlife of punishment, never, not once.

In my heart, I was just a naturally cooperative, friendly, usually cheerful pastor; an affectionate, faithful husband; and a reasonably knowledgeable, suburban gardener, not even an active member of our homeowners' association on Carlton Street. The bishop did not ask me for my theological opinions. The sexton knew that I would always forget to turn out the lights in the sacristy. Candy told me regularly that I knew next to nothing about how to properly cook a steak. I did not golf particularly well. I had no financial prowess that would make a fortune for me on the stock exchange. I was average in every way. I was vanilla pudding in the salad bar of life.

And then, suddenly, without preamble, I was compelled to stand and fight for something. This trip was not an academic exercise. There I was on the *Grand Rapina*, trying to summon up courage that I was certain I did not have, in order to protect the vulnerable and the exploited. I had no inner resources for that. I was brave only under duress. I'm not sure that even counts at all. I often worried that I would manage to embarrass God, if he tried to count on somebody like me.

But, as Candace said, we did have to eat.

The ship's Captain stood up from his dinner table when he saw us coming. It was an inauthentic demonstration of respect for Candace and myself, and for God. Moze Balodis was clean shaven and manicured and pampered in his formal attire, and his jet-black hair was slicked down like an arctic seal's, with a pomade that smelled distinctly floral, like licorice. Up close, I could see that the man had terrible teeth. Had icebergs on the ocean kept him away from the dentist? Or was his soul so rotten, filling up his person with evil, that it was overflowing and falling out of his mouth?

As we approached our captor, I thought of stabbing Moze in his sleek seal's neck, and in my mind's eye I could see the jagged hole that I could inflict next to his jugular. The blood would ooze down the front of his starched jacket, first thin like wine, and then thick like liqueur. Knives for cutlery were strewn all over the tabletop, sparkling in their open-air accessibility. I could quickly grab one and pounce. Even a small stab wound could prove fatal, I thought, if skillfully placed. Captain Balodis had thought so little of our ability to defend ourselves that he had left actual weapons lying around, underestimating our canniness to use them. He would not look so proud after a good knifing, I thought. Oh, how could I *think* of such a thing?

"Pastor and Mrs. Atterley, how kind of you to join me."

Candace and I sat down. The table had been set in sterling silver flatware and fine crystal and china. A centerpiece of orchids drooped languorously. Under the frightful circumstances, who had been sent to get flowers, of all things? Delicacies warmed under shining, handled domes. Champagne bottles cooled in icy buckets. I thought that I smelled roasted turkey. A statuesque, buxom blonde woman stood nearby in the shadows of the furniture, just out of sight. She was the waitress for the dinner, and doubtless part sentry, and probably also dessert for Captain Balodis at midnight.

"I have called you here to discuss the terms of your employment," the Captain began in his Baltic resonance. He spoke as if I were receiving job coaching. "As you have no doubt seen, we are gathering Latin America's castoffs, and these souls will require spiritual care while they cruise with us."

"I wouldn't call it cruising."

"I would like for you to understand that the *Grand Rapina* has been commissioned by our benefactor, Mr. Walker Masterson, as a ship of mercy. We are entrusted with a special task. We are developing a vaccine, a boon to mankind, which our passengers will generously contribute to by giving their blood in a perfectly clinical, highly professional setting. Our goal is to eradicate poverty over the Earth."

Candace took my hand under the table.

"You, Pastor Atterley, are to prepare these guests with calm virtues before their blood is drawn. Of course, you will also work to prepare them to meet their God, should an unpredictable accident happen, for our research into these areas is new. Things happen, though we try to be careful." The Captain motioned to the waitress for his dinner. "You will keep our guests in a sedate frame of mind, which is necessary in order to harvest their blood in a form most useful as a base for a vaccine." Captain Balodis took a sip of his champagne. "Anxiety produces hormones that affect the research. These complicate the work. The scientists complain." He tapped his mouth with his napkin. "Do you understand, Pastor Atterley?"

"I think I do. You want me to make sure nobody causes any trouble."

Captain Balodis smiled shrewdly. "You could put it that way, yes."

"And you want me to convince these poor people that God approves of what you are about to do to them."

"You need not be so cynical, Pastor. We are creating a vaccine to better the world. God also wants a better world, correct?"

"Why use a minister to do your dirty work? You could just drug them all, make them unconscious. Then they wouldn't be hard to handle, now would they?"

The Captain sliced his entree. It was venison, not turkey. "The experts have considered the options, Pastor. They determined that these kinds of refugees have greater faith in God than most. They'll turn to him, and you, for help, and will not need the extra medicine. Their faith will steady them and make them, how do you say, compliant."

"Which makes everything cheaper for you. More profits?"

"Expenses are a matter of concern, naturally."

"One pastor's cruise fare is cheaper than sedating a mob."

"And more practical. Medicine wears off. Faith does not."

"Do you understand that you're about to commit murders? That people won't live through this?"

"No, we are creating a vaccine to eliminate poverty."

"I think you mean you're creating a vaccine to eliminate the impoverished people, not poverty."

"Poverty resides in poor people, does it not?"

"I've been a prisoner in my cabin for weeks. What if I say no?"

"Then I will be forced to conclude that instead of fulfilling the services for which we negotiated your contract, you have decided on the higher service of being the first person to contribute his blood in the interest of this marvelous goal of science." Moze Balodis glared at me over his plate. His venison bled into a pool of creamy juices.

"You murderous bastard!"

"May I suggest that you calm down and eat? You will need your strength for all of your shepherding."

My Candace stood up. "You're a brute! We'll live to see your corpse!"

Captain Balodis laughed. He motioned again to his giant Swedish concubine. "It seems that my guests are not hungry. What a pity! Please return them to their beautiful suite."

The blonde slid out of the dining room soundlessly and returned with Chris Adamos, our minder. This time, he came with rope for our hands. They bound us.

"The work begins once we clear the Panama Canal, Pastor Atterley. I trust you will be ready," Moze said.

"I won't go quietly. I'll do everything I can to stop you."

Chris bound my wife and me tightly for our walk through the dining room, elevators, and hallways. He was not so sure, now, that he would be safe from our attack, so he took precautions. He released us by slitting the rope in front of our stateroom and pushing us inside, like convicts. I went in the bathroom and vomited on my knees, and Candace, though royal in her heart, mopped up the mess with a towel.

We sat up all night on our twinkling balcony, praying for help as the waves churned with unsettled energy below us. We wondered briefly if we should end our long life together by jumping off into the frigid sea, in a pact of refusal to participate in hurting the refugees, God's children. There was no point in screaming. There was no point in crying. Strangely, there was little to be said. Unless a holy angel came to rescue us, we would remain prisoners on the *Grand Rapina*. Without having any dinner at all, which I would not have been able to keep down, anyway, we waited for dawn.

As I prepare for my trial, I force myself to recall the horror on the faces of the refugees when they understood that they had been tricked. They looked at me in anguish, as if they believed that I had been a party to their hoodwinking. They seemed to think that God should kill me on the spot for betraying them, and when God did not, the people were inconsolable. They clung to one another, or hid their dark eyes, or turned them woefully up to the heavens, and their infants cried out in bereft, tearless screams. Still, their respect for the Lord was so great that they dared not lay their hands on a man of God to extract revenge.

It was at this time that I revealed to the runaways that I, and my wife, were also prisoners. I walked among the refugees to try to give them an encouraging word. Emmie walked with me. We looked for the young girl who had been in hiding with her kidnapper, but they were no longer onboard. They had been spirited on, and spirited off as well, probably in the chaos at Colon. To this day, I pray for that child and can barely refrain from wishing the worst fire and brimstone to fall upon her captor.

When I next blessed the refugees on the hideous Starlight Deck, I reached up and pulled my clerical collar off. I did not want to incriminate God in what I was about to do.

* * *

Dr. Jenny Elihu and First Officer Anthony Vera were enjoying a long kiss on the upper deck. They'd been meeting there clandestinely for weeks, enjoying the privacy and the booze that had been left in the bar. Jenny Elihu could really put it away, but no one would have accused her of needing to be numbed from a flagellated conscience.

"Your eyes, they look so fantastic, like iridescent, smoky quartz in the Caribbean sun!"

"Come on, Tony, stop the fake Spanish accent. I know you're from Hoboken. Did you leave the Captain in the bridge to steer this thing?"

"Not to worry. It's all automated now."

"Are you ready? It won't be long."

"Of course. But you're the one with the pressure. All those people. All that blood."

"It's what I signed up for. I have to pay off my college debts somehow." Jenny threw back her vodka shots. "This job pays more money than I've ever seen in my life, and I might get to publish research, once the notoriety dies down." Jenny looped her fingers playfully into the First Officer's belt. "People will forget. They always do."

"They'll forget *if* you don't get caught."

"No, it doesn't matter. Eventually, people won't care."

"Spoken like a true cynic." Tony Vera let himself be pulled nearer to Dr. Elihu.

"How do you want to get started?"

Tony nuzzled Jenny's neck. "At the sound of the church bells, they'll come. I'm going to broadcast cathedral bells over the loud speaker, and tell them to meet Atterley in the chapel. He's going to pray over them and do whatever it is that he does."

"Then what?"

"You know what. Then they're going to get a spa treatment and a swim. You designed the procedure yourself, Doctor."

"After that, send them down to me about two dozen at a time. I'll draw their blood. It's a production line."

"Will do."

"And dry them off first. I don't want to stand in their stinking puddles."

"Everyone will get a towel. What, do you think I'm uncivilized?"

Tony and Jenny put their heads together and laughed.

"Now, why don't you come and let me help you relax in my stateroom?" Tony ran his fingers over Jenny's cheek. "You're going to make history and help the whole world!"

"I'm going to pay off my Toyota, first."

"If you insist."

Tony grabbed Jenny by the waist, and they disappeared together into the officer's quarters. Afterward, they plotted together in the shower, blowing soap bubbles at each other.

* * *

Downstairs in a dark and vacant ballroom on the Starlight Deck, the dusty refugees slept the sleep of the hopeful. Husbands and wives held hands as they dozed, not dreading to give the mere drop of blood that would pay for their passage to a better life. Children dreamed of clean water and new friends and toys stacked in colorful piles up to the sky. Grandmothers' old lips said thanks to the Virgin Mary for their deliverance. Grandfathers' old lips said thanks for the grandmothers. Even the birds and the dogs and the snakes curled together in a warm and peaceful reverie, with the pet snakes providing their coiled skins as pillows for the puppies, and the macaws sheltering plump rabbits under their outstretched, indigo wings. There was rest. Pastor James Atterley had not explained his horrifying captivity to them yet, nor tearfully confessed their fate.

In the windowless ballroom, the refugees could not see or hear the alterations underway in the Sunrise Pool, where specialized technicians prepared the free-flowing saltwater space for the treatments. The entire pool was drained, deepened by four feet, and sanitized. Sensors for motion detection and body fluids were installed. Underwater cameras were networked and steadied. Temperature controls were bypassed and rerouted. A video recording system was threaded through an opaque roof that blocked out the sun and muffled the noise. Stadium seating around the pool that would have given a clear view of the activities from the adjacent spa was completely torn down and replaced with partitions.

A baptism of death was about to transpire.

There would be the ringing of bells and the crying of owls.

CHAPTER SEVEN

Shortly after sunup the next morning, I heard the door to our cabin open as a master key was inserted from the hallway. The noise awoke me out of an ash-colored doze, and when roused I had a moment when I wasn't sure where I was. Oh, yes. Imprisoned on a cruise ship. The recollection shot through me with a force that contracted my legs, awakening me in a state of panic. When I remembered that I was confined, I turned over on the bed and reached for my wife, scooping her to my chest, and hoping that she did not feel my fright. Candy's presence anchored me emotionally, restoring my strength. I managed to stand up.

Rumpled in yesterday's disrespectful clothes, which I'd not bothered to remove, I walked sleepily to the cabin door just as it swung open, dodging a rattling metal cart with three breakfasts on it that was wheeled into our suite by an unshaven Chris Adamos. At this early hour, his silhouette was illuminated by the apricot sunrise streaming in from the hallway, giving him a spectral outline. He parked the food in front of the television, stepped on a creaky wheel to lock the cart into place, and turned away as if to go about his other wretched errands. In the half light, I could see that Chris didn't appear to have slept very much, either. He was slovenly and mumbling to himself.

"They still get the good food, keep them alive, Captain's orders," Chris griped under his breath. "Forget cold oatmeal. Don't let it happen again." We were an imposition to our zookeeper as he threw in meat for the animals, and he was upset about the cost of our upkeep, as if it came out of his personal salary. Or was he jealous because of his own meager rations? No Vasodilator Diet for Candy and me. It seemed that the Captain had reprimanded the steward for depriving us. Chris Adamos was in trouble, and losing sleep over it.

But he surprised me by coming right back inside with young Emmie, whom he gripped by one of her delicate arms. "Your interpreter," Chris muttered, pulling the girl into our stateroom. "The Captain said to keep her happy. She's needed. Can't find her parents. Been bawling her eyes out." Chris then locked the cabin door again from the outside, and disappeared down the corridor.

Candy sat up on the bed. She and I looked at each other in bafflement. Out of the blue we had a child on our hands. At one point, that had been our lives' greatest desire.

"What's going on? Do you know this little girl?"

"Yes, she helps me when I go downstairs to hear confessions."

Emmie's eyes were swollen and she was heaving tears. Her arms bore the red welts of having been roughed up by Chris Adamos. "I can't find mama, they made me come here! I want to go home!" Emmie wept. She promptly ran to Candy with outstretched arms, intuitively trusting her. Hysterical and confused, the child clung to my wife, alternating between shouting into her face and frantically pointing toward the cabin door.

Candace quickly wrapped the child up in her bedspread. "It's all right, it's all right," my wife soothed. "You're safe." She smoothed the girl's brown hair and rocked her. Candy looked over at me with a questioning gaze. "What should I do?"

I knelt down to be at eye level with Emmie. "I want to tell you a secret. My wife and I know we can't go home right now, either. But we're going to figure out a way to do that, and we're going to help you, too. Until then, you just stay close to us."

Candy began to wipe the child's nose. "How did you learn English?" my wife asked as she dabbed with her tissue. "Did you learn in school?"

Emmie glanced at the eggs and bacon on the tray nearby.

Candy saw at once. "Here, sit down and eat," my wife offered. She cleared the desk of the stationery on which she'd been composing her onerous will, and arranged Emmie in a chair and pushed her up close to the food. It was a maternal gesture that I found touching, part of all of those nesting and mothering instincts that Candy had never been able to express. "This will make you feel better. Do you like fried eggs? Don't worry, honey, we'll find your family." Emmie rubbed her sore eyes with her fists and tasted the food. She ate a strip of bacon with trembling hands, and thirstily drank down the orange juice that now seemed so luxurious in its beauty and refreshment, to people who'd had nothing to eat for hours.

My wife was also extremely hungry, and these were the perfect circumstances for her to get a migraine. I prepared a plate and a cup for Candace and brought them to her. "Here, this is for you. Eat up!" She waved the coffee away, but gratefully took the eggs and toast.

For myself, I drank eagerly from the thermos carafe of cold water that had been brought for us. It galled me, but I had to partake of the nutrition that had been wheeled into our captivity. I felt light headed and faint. I consumed the sausage links and potatoes as if they might be my last meal. I resisted the thought that maybe I didn't want to live anymore, anyway.

Unexpectedly, I heard the clank and roar of heavy machinery. The *Grand Rapina* had sailed on from Colon and had entered the first lock in the Panama Canal on the Atlantic side. As the rising sunshine began to brighten our journey, through the drapes I saw the narrow, two-lane cleft in the water of Gatun Locks through which the *Grand Rapina* would be threaded, and I knew that our nearly fifty-mile isthmus voyage to the cruise ship dock at Fuerte Amador on the Pacific side of Panama had begun.

At these Gatun Locks, I could see that we were being carefully tethered and attended by specially designed tugboats dragging cables attached to the ship to keep it from colliding with the sides of the Canal, and to take stresses off of the *Grand Rapina*'s own propulsion systems. As each of the locks slowly filled, the *Grand Rapina* would be lifted indiscernibly about one hundred feet up, over the Continental Divide in the man-made, freshwater Gatun Lake, where we would sail through marked channels over its wide waters to the Culebra Cut. After passing through that narrow and dangerous gorge, we would press on to come out of the Pedro Miguel Locks that marked the mid-way point, gradually descending, and finally return to sea level at the Miraflores Locks on the Pacific side, exiting the Panama Canal.

I later learned that thousands and thousands of workers had died to carve this aquatic marvel, a combination of human engineering genius and the simple functions of gravity. The workers had been grievously harassed by everything from disease-carrying mosquitoes to tropical mudslides that buried them alive to gruesome accidents that forever maimed them. In an effort prior to that of the Americans, the valiant French had given up digging in disgust and left the region, leaving the U.S. Army Corps of Engineers and allied experts to begin again with the scarred jungle project. The situation was so dire that the adjacent Panama Railroad rolled away carrying multitudes of dead workers every day for years.

This railroad was critical to the eventual success of building the Panama Canal. After intense diplomatic negotiations between America and Columbia, the railway was built fifty years earlier than the Panama Canal in an entrepreneurial spirit by a United States in the grip of the California Gold Rush and eager to connect both its coasts with the latest railroad and steam technologies. The railroad's construction was over old Spanish trade paths; through swamps writhing with snakes, tempestuous rivers, and torrential downpours; and amidst riotous cholera, malaria, and yellow fever outbreaks, suffered in ferocious heat and humidity. These miseries also resulted in the deaths of scores of workers who came from all over the world. Many of these ragged emigrants, sadly, had come to work on the Panama Railway in hopes of making enough money to move on to California themselves, to prospect for gold.

Why do so many people always have to die?

As Candace, Emmie, and I ate, my stomach tensed at an incongruous sound that I will never forget. It blocked out the busy shouts of the workers calling to one another outside in the Control House above the lock's highest chamber. Sacred music on the *Grand Rapina*? I heard the loveliest electronic church bells chiming. Broadcast over the intercom system, throughout the entire ship, presumably, came the melodious ringing. Next came a curt announcement. "All guests, please assemble in the chapel. All guests, please assemble in the chapel," came the summons in English. It was then repeated in Spanish.

I laid down my fork. I cannot describe the degree of dread that I felt. I suppose that I could have refused to leave our state room, but that would have meant certain execution for us, including for Emmie. In the middle of trying to stave off hunger, I felt whatever honor I possessed meld with my resolve. Yes, this time I would perform an hour-long worship service, but not for the purposes that Captain Balodis demanded. I looked again at my plate. The steward was very nervous that we eat. An idea began to form.

I looked in the mirror. My color was pale, but my eyes were clear. This morning, I'd not yet bathed or even brushed my teeth. Hastily, I did take time to change my clothes. I then braced myself to perform my pastoral duties. Hygiene seemed the least of my worries.

Candace ran a brush through her hair. Then she turned to comb the child's.

I saw Emmanuella stuff a corner of buttered toast into her pocket. She, also, feared hunger. Had she already become acquainted with it in her few years?

Chris Adamos came back and immediately made a mockery of politeness by knocking on our cabin door with great officiousness. My wife and I could never anticipate when he would restrain us, since it seemed to be a matter of his mood and sense of danger at the moment, but this time Chris had no rope with which to bind our hands. Looking back, I realize that he could not have bound us, for the refugees would have instantly reacted to the sight.

Now that there was a sizable number of "guests," a real crowd, Chris seemed to think that he had better escort me with some fanfare. I don't know if he wanted the adulation that came with our bleak celebrity, or if he wanted to demonstrate to his lurking superiors that he was keeping our bodies and souls together with adequate food. This event would be my first full-length performance, according to Chris; there would be no more short confessions and simple blessings. I would no longer try to answer in the fleetest of moments "Why am I sick? Why am I poor?" This day, I had better deliver, or else. "You're needed downstairs right now," Chris said. And then, almost chummily, "Are you ready for the show? Don't be nervous. You've got a full house."

I gathered my Bible, and, for some reason, three or four ink pens. Filling my hands made me feel more prepared. I'd had so much to deal with, of course I'd written no sermon. I trusted that the words would come, perhaps as memories from my years in the pulpit, and I relied on decades of experience as a man of the cloth under the inspiration of the Holy Spirit. I mulled over what Captain Balodis had said about how I must placate and reassure the refugees by the misuse of the Gospel. I must maintain that they were in the middle of God's will for them. I must make them believe that all was well. There were to be no anxious hormones in their bloodstreams. Dr. Jenny Elihu would be sure to punish me if I made her ghoulish work more difficult. My sole purpose for being kept alive was to make the blood drawing easy for *her*.

Candace and Emmanuella held hands, and we all followed Chris to an elevator, riding down morosely to the area that the *Grand Rapina*'s crew referred to as "the chapel." Something was being worshipped there, but it was not God. To my eye, the room was actually an auditorium, not the small, intimate space that the word "chapel" typically connotes. The room looked to me as if it could seat several hundred people. The space was brightly lit. The ceiling was coffered and mounted with equipment for sound and projection. The auditorium contained a deep, wooden stage with a dais, with a heavy cotton curtain hanging over it in symmetrical pleats. A large projection screen, which I would not need, was unfurled in front of the curtain.

I made my way down a slight incline to the stage in front. No cross, no altar, no offering plates, no kneeling rail, no communion bread or cups of wine, nothing graced this "chapel" to identify it as a Christian place of worship. I might have been the speaker at a meeting of the local Rotary Club. I stood there and looked at the auditorium. I could also see my wrinkled knuckles turning white while I gripped the podium, containing my rage in my angry squeeze. These were gardener's hands, skilled in bringing life, not death. I intended to keep them that way.

I dedicated the lackluster, secular space to the Lord as best I could in my heart, and opened my Bible to the first chapter of the book of John. This reading was for me, not the "guests." "The light shines in the darkness, and the darkness has not overcome it," I read. I closed my eyes and repeated these words. I clung to them like a castaway, and felt their subtle defiance of the power of evil. Now, more than ever in my life, I needed to be on the side of the light, the holy light, God's light.

And then, the pitiful, desperate escapees filed in from the Starlight Deck, just under a hundred souls in this first group, I gauged. They were every shade of brown and black, every age, and their disheveled, humble clothes were a striking contrast to the opulence of the cruise ship. Their farmers' fingertips dirtied the pale, velvet-covered walls. Their heavy work boots soiled the sapphire carpets with mud. But their eyes were aglow with hope. I could see this optimism even from the stage. Truly believing that they were going to church, the refugees were quiet and orderly and respectful, shushing their babies and filling in the room with barely a rustle. No, they did not yet know.

Crew members brought the refugees inside this auditorium through a set of double doors and guided them to rows of swiveling, padded chairs, as if they were invited to see a movie in a theater. My breath caught in my throat as I watched. I grieved that the refugees were being deceived. On the surface, yes, one could say that I participated knowingly in the charade, but I had a plan to resist it. I was no co-conspirator. I was as wise as a serpent, but aspired to be a liberating dove.

While they must have understood that their attendance was mandatory, these runaways, many of whom were devout and faithful believers, had no problem whatsoever when they were told that every one of their days aboard the *Grand Rapina* would begin with a Christian service.

The refugees of other faiths, or of no faith at all, who were mixed in among the Christian believers must have thought of the service as sort of a political rally, given by the party they didn't want to join, but which, as a practical matter, controlled their free ship's passage and hence could not be offended. Thus, these unbelievers filed in cooperatively, as well.

As the refugees were guided inside by the crew, they sat down in the rows of comfortable chairs. I could tell by their discreet smiles that some of the runaways thought that these chairs were only the beginning of their new, vastly upgraded way of life. There was little conversation, as if the people were subdued in anticipation. I wondered if Emmanuella's family might be in this group, but judging by the child's reaction as her eyes scanned the crowd, her relatives were not present. Soon, the auditorium was completely filled. Candy and Emmie also found seats. Crew members stood by the chapel's doors, locking them together, and shortly the workers signaled for me to begin. I motioned to Emmie. She got up from her seat and came to my side without fear. How brave she was! "All you have to do is repeat in Spanish everything that I say. I won't make it hard. Don't be afraid."

"OK," the girl answered. "I'll try."

I closed my eyes and said a silent prayer to God. I remembered that at the very beginning of this *Grand Rapina* misadventure, I had wanted to sail on the high seas in part to emulate the life of Saint Paul. I then turned to the book of Acts, to Chapter 16, to the story of Paul and his traveling companion, Silas, who were in chains in a prison in Philippi, Greece. One of the reasons that I loved this story was that Paul had made his captors publicly admit that they had mistreated and abused he and Silas, and Paul demanded his civil rights. He refused to go quietly from the scene of the mistreatment, refused to make his oppressors feel less anxious when they discovered with trepidation that Paul was a Roman citizen with Empire rights to a fair trial. Paul forced his captors to acknowledge what they had done. He stood up for himself and for his companion, and so would I.

"I am going to speak this morning on the topic of social justice."

The crew members guarding the doors immediately squirmed. Good, I thought. Let me put some fear into them for a change. What did they expect, a sermon about the meekness of a flock of sheep? Perhaps a discourse on humility?

I looked out on the crowd of souls assembled before me. I worried for them, and tried my best to speak to what I felt was their greatest need. I wanted to issue a warning to them, subtly, to alert them about what was to come on the *Grand Rapina*. The refugees were in good spirits, however, still believing that they were finally headed toward their new way of life. They weren't expecting some kind of clandestine signal. So, I decided to keep my comments broadly symbolic. At the right time, the candle of the Lord would enlighten the people and bring them the understanding that they needed. This I had to believe.

Here is how I began, to the best of my memory. I hope that my trial judges will hear my pastor's heart in these words:

"Sometimes in life, we find ourselves in chains of physical or emotional bondage. I, myself, know this feeling. Usually, at the bottom of the terrible detention is hatred."

I paused to let Emmanuella catch up and gain confidence. She translated and then waited for me to go on. I could almost feel the child maturing as she stood at my elbow.

"As a minister and fellow human being, I could stand here all day and never fully explain the complex nature of hatred and the injustice that it brings. Let me only try to sum up two of its primary traits. First, hatred is almost always rooted in willful ignorance. There are those who will never want to know us for who we really are. They prefer to live with darkened minds, and they will find even the fact that we exist too much to bear."

I let my words sink in.

"Consider, for instance, the example of Paul and Silas in prison. These men were hauled before the magistrates in Philippi for expressing religious ideas that some people of the town found objectionable. Many people, even today, still find unfamiliar ideas and people who look a little different from them to be threats to their community. And these fearful ones still do not want to gather to talk about our differences, to try to work together in brotherhood and sisterhood, which might turn into many occasions for hospitality, understanding, and friendship.

"This brings me to the second aspect of hatred. It is always unreasonable in its insistence on having its own way. Hatred refuses to acknowledge the worthiness of those who disagree with it. Hatred believes itself superior and rebuffs compromise. So, those of us who are excluded from society's acknowledgement are going to have to claim our rights, as Saint Paul did, and demand a good and safe place in God's world, for there are many who would take those blessings away from us without a second thought, with the intent to wipe us out. How we choose to insist on having a place in the world will be our life's work. Let us choose a path of love and not hate."

The crowd stirred as I spoke. One grandmother in the front row closed her crinkly eyes and whispered to herself. One young man in the back stood to raise his hands in praise to God. A crew member gruffly made him sit down.

"Today, you might find yourself in an economic prison. You might be in an emotional prison. You might be in a relational prison. You have chosen a way of escape on the *Grand Rapina*. But above all else, you must realize that as for Paul and Silas, and for all of us, it takes God's help to escape from a prison, and that help will often come in unexpected ways. For example, an elderly, gardening pastor stands before you now, willing to offer assistance."

I paused to collect my thoughts. Emmie finished her sentence.

"The final observation that I want to leave you with today is this: The Lord of the Universe does not like unjust incarceration, of any kind. His work of breaking down prisons is messy, dangerous, inconvenient, and never really complete on this Earth. As we attempt to help God in his work of dismantling prisons, you will sometimes feel the crush of the bricks as they inevitably fall on you. But take heart! God knows how to set you free!"

In my passion, I felt the color rise in my face. Instinctively, I felt for my clerical collar, which I no longer wore. I did not want it in any way to be seen as a show of rank. No matter. The Lord was not concerned with my wardrobe.

"In this world, I am only a prisoner, just like you. I am your equal in the need for Divine deliverance. Let us work toward it, together! Amen."

Emmie looked over to me to see if I were done speaking. I have to say that she was a bit dazzled. I hoped that I came across as a fervent Christian, because for the first time in my life I was vibrating like an old-style Marxist. I had agitated publicly for social justice, in my own modest way, and the sensation was new to me. I nodded to Emmie that I was done and closed my Bible.

I collected Candy and Emmie and attempted to exit with the crowd. As I tried to leave, a crew member who seemed especially annoyed by my talk, a muscular, aggressive woman, held her arm over the doorway, barring my departure. The woman was large-hipped and broad-shouldered and mean, like a prison matron. She shook her big bony head. "No, you stay here. Wait for a call from the medical center."

"We want to leave right now. Let us out!"

The woman reached up and poked my collarbone with her forefinger, emphasizing her point. "You stay put! You'll leave when I say you can leave!"

"Get out of our way!"

The woman exploded at me. "You're going to stand right here while they're hosed off in the spa, and then prepped in the pool, at which point Your Majesty is going down there and mop up the blood after it's drawn!" she screamed. "Any questions?"

Candace turned an incandescent shade of red, all five feet, five inches of her. "You get your hands off my husband, or I'll scratch your eyes out!"

My wife's words came back in a horrifying boomerang, as the crew member gripped my dear Candy by the throat, throttling her with both hands, and shoving her backward over a chair.

"James!" Candace tried to call out, clawing at the woman's face.

Suddenly, Chris Adamos crashed in through the double doors, realizing that his time playing hooky in guarding us was about to cost him his job. "Oh my god, Hazel, you're killing her!" he bellowed, grabbing the prison matron by her hair. "Let her go, or we're both fish food! Let her go!"

The large woman backed off. Emmie pushed by her to hug Candace.

I rushed to my darling wife's side. Already, I could see the purple imprints of the assailant's fingers glowing on Candy's neck. I was absolutely furious. "No matter what happens, I'll make sure you get what you deserve!" I held my wife as she caught her breath.

"If I'd had my rolling pin, she'd never have touched me!"

It was a good sign. My Candace still had so much life left in her!

Chris Adamos did not have the nerve to bind our hands as he took us back to our cabin. He was flustered that Candy had been attacked and that the preacher's talk had ended in a brawl, and he probably feared that Captain Moze Balodis would find out that he'd been napping while we were in the chapel. Chris escorted us back to our room with profuse apologies. A half an hour later, chastened, he came carrying a large apple pie and a tub of vanilla ice cream. Emmie's eyes grew wide with desire. It was a small bribe, but my womenfolk ate it. As for me, I let Chris know that I would not eat another bite until we were allowed to wander freely from the suite that had become our prison. He blanched at my words. "Please, eat!" he begged. "I don't want to have to tell the doctor!"

I never saw Chris Adamos again.

Candace, Emmie, and I spent the remaining afternoon playing a board game that we pulled down from the top shelf in our closet. Our room's previous occupants had apparently been fans of *Sorry*. When nightfall came, Candy and I made up a little cot for Emmie, and we hung a beach towel over the rolling luggage cart for her, like a room divider, so that she would have her own private space within our state room.

And the evening and the morning were Emmie's first day with us.

* * *

Later that night, under cover of darkness, two restaurant workers dumped the refugees' dinner garbage off of the back of the *Grand Rapina* into Lake Gatun. They also had a lumpy and bloody bundle to dispose of, meat that Chef Danilo had butchered himself. The young men were both from the coffee plantations of Guatemala, and were trying to get ahead by indenturing themselves to Majestic Waves.

"Can you gag down that Vasodilator Diet? I thought we'd get good chow on this boat," a waiter for the Sky on Reserve complained.

"They say it makes their veins expand or something like that, to make pulling out the blood a lot easier," the assistant cook replied nonchalantly.

"But I didn't know I had to eat that crap, too."

"You keep your mouth shut, or they'll be yanking at your veins."

"Hand me that trash can. Let's hurry up and get this over with."

"You can't be in a rush, man. You got no schedule anymore. We're on this boat for nine whole months. That's what the contract says."

"Just long enough for my girl to push out that little baby I made. That's how I wound up on this dump. I got a kid to support!"

"Me, I'm saving to open a store. I'm a businessman, really, an entrepreneur. I want to sell cold drinks and chips to the tourists, maybe some discount perfumes. After this trip, no more cruise ship slavery for me!"

"Here, hand me that sack of meat. Chef said it was spoiled already when he cut it up."

"It stinks like rotten pig! Throw it over, get rid of it!"

As the package was flung into the lake, a small patch of cloth slipped unnoticed from its confines. The square name patch read "Adamos" in a handsome embroidered script, but the patch was not seen in the dark as the crew members hurriedly finished their chores to return to the lower decks where they lodged.

"Well, there goes the last of the prime rib," the junior cook said wistfully over the splash. "They'd have killed me if I'd been the one to let it spoil. Danilo got off."

106

"See you in Fuerte Amador in the morning! Sleep well, my friend. I hope Luis cleaned the bed bugs up."

Smiling crocodiles quickly gobbled their monogrammed snack. They slowly winked their reptilian eyes, thrashed their spiked tails, and dove to the bottom of the rainforest waters.

CHAPTER EIGHT

We had been delayed overnight by the backlog of cargo ships crowding the Gatun Lake watershed, but at last we briefly lay anchor in Fuerte Amador on the Pacific side. We had come the full transit of the Panama Canal, skimming locks, dodging submerged mountains, and, thanks to our Captain's treacherous skills, stealing over the waters like a wraith and attracting little attention. Moze Balodis' goal seemed to be to escape into the unobstructed Pacific, where he would have room to maneuver the *Grand Rapina* with less chance of being observed.

Since it accessed the ocean, I could see a mile-long causeway in Panama Bay that connected four small islands, a marina, and the ubiquitous malls and restaurants aimed at tourists. As it sped out of the marina, I was surprised to see a sign from home: the flag of the Ditkins Institute flying on a small boat bound for the nearby tropical research center. Panama City was just a few miles away, and I could see a glint of its modern glass skyscrapers glittering on the horizon in the steamy, sweltering heat. I wondered if refugees from that capital would find a way to flock to the *Grand Rapina*, and if they would feel the need to surreptitiously flee. If they did, like most of the others, they would have to be brought by clandestine tenders.

But Captain Balodis had other plans. He did not stay long in Fuerte Amador, only long enough to allow Dr. Elihu to begin the dreadful work for which they'd been hired by Majestic Waves. Instead, he sailed the *Grand Rapina* into the open ocean, rushed south by the untamed Pacific coastline of Columbia, sped over the equator with the whales breaching nearby, and made haste to the naturally deep Puerto de Manta in Ecuador. The sun was brutally hot as the age-old Montecristi Mountain came into view, and then the expansive peninsula, but the busy trawlers in the harbor were not deterred by the burning blaze. Single-minded, the wooden boats were on their way to unload their catches of tuna, marlin, and shark for the canneries, which dotted the coast. Then, the crews would probably wander on to the cafes for cold beers, or maybe to their hammocks for rest, out of the sun. How I longed to have been born a simple fisherman.

The morning that we learned that all of our food was gone, and that Captain Balodis had refused to bring provisions from the plentiful fish, vegetable, and banana markets in Manta, I nearly gave up. There had even been chocolate to buy in Manta, made just for joy. Moze did not want to be interrupted in the middle of his dastardly project, for fear of being caught. He brought the *Grand Rapina* back out into the waters of the Pacific Ocean, with no intention of turning back. Why had he even bothered to lay anchor? I think in the dangerous, crime-ridden port of Manta, he must have had a scare. A blackmailer, maybe?

In upcoming days, I discovered that Dr. Elihu watched on a console of security cameras in the medical center as the refugees were brought down from the chapel into the spa. The doctor had instructed the crew to hose down the refugees there to keep them from befouling the sanitized basin that was their next stop, a malevolent swimming pool where their "treatments" would begin. Once the sunny site where well-off families gathered to take in cool splashes under blue skies and puffing clouds, the pool was now like a state-of-the-art, shrouded volcano into which live sacrificial victims would be tossed.

To begin with, there was no more sky. I can only guess that the purpose for blocking out the sun was to prevent observers from watching the macabre activities, on the small chance that some crew members on the *Grand Rapina* would object to them. The impression that the overarching shadows left was that everything that happened inside the pool was nobody's business. I can't say that no expense was spared to keep out the revealing light, because the cheap opaque panels that were used like shingles implied that no one would care what took place, so why go to the trouble of ensuring complete secrecy with expensive building materials?

Looking back, I wonder now, too, if the theft of the sky was intended to rob the refugees of their attachment to the Divine in their lives, to remove from them any impulse to send heavenward their cries for intervention, or (perhaps especially) their demands for vengeance. Taking away the blue sky took away God's watchfulness in the calculating minds of those tasked with cowing the runaways, and left the refugees in a physical space that felt impenetrably void of a sacred presence. Such was the result of stealing the light: It blocked out God.

Sometimes at night, I can almost walk in the flesh of a frightened brown man being dragged into the chilling pool. I imagine myself looking up at the walls around me, fearing what was about to occur. I think that I would have wondered what I had done in my life that had made me such an object of scorn, by people I did not even know, that they would think me nothing more than a rat that must be cornered and drowned.

After all, a god had made the rat's spirit and a god had made the pool's waters, and, like them, I believed that I was good and welcome in a god's world. I think that I would have waited for help from this god. He would let the rat live. He would come down as the great, green sea turtle floating astride a spacious, hollow log, and he would open the top of the filling volcano and swim the poor rat to safety on top of the earth, to see the sight of the sun and the sky once again. The god of the rat would come. He would come down. But no.

I think that my last thoughts would have been of surprise that the life spirits of a god would permit my mistreatment. In my last moments of feeling the warmth of rat flesh and the flex of rat bones, I would have been so achingly, immeasurably disappointed that some god, my god, any god, allowed the absolute, unfettered violence that finally took my life while I still waited for rescue with a faint wish of hope. A god did not respond to rat pleas or rat tears or rat pain. I was only a lowly rat, after all.

Then, I would have turned from this absent god, crying but not begging, realizing that there was no help in all of the world, nor in all of the stars, not for me, and I would have hastened my death with deep gulps of the frothing weapon that gushed, because sleep would have been the only merciful quietude from the cumulative abuse that had been my whole beleaguered, brown-skinned, rat's life, and the inexplicable, implacable cause of the end of it. And as my soul departed from my heart, how shocked I would have been to see that even my death was not enough for my oppressors, as they drained the drowned rat of his lifeblood and poured it into a crystal vial to kill his rat kindred, too.

My god, the rat mourns.

Is it a spiritual gift to be able to feel another person's agony? If so, I pray that the Lord would take such a gift away from me, because my sanity wanes. Those who died in the pool on the *Grand Rapina* no longer feel pain, but I live with the throbbing memory of their loss every day. To forestall insanity, and to do what I can to bring justice, all I can do is to tell without adornment what happened on that wicked ocean liner. I believe that I must do the telling now, before the tale sears my tongue as with a hot coal.

No angel of God came to shield my awareness. But, like the prophet Daniel, though I was aware, full of the knowledge of what was to come, I still did not understand. With my physical and spiritual senses, I could see what was unfolding on the *Grand Rapina*, but I did not know what to do about it. Like the raptor owl, I could look clearly into the darkness, but I was the captive, I was the prey, I was the prisoner.

Let my trial judges make a record, while I can still speak.

The refugees came quietly to the spa, at first. It was only at the foot of the stairs (they did not use the elevators) that the guides suddenly turned on the people and seized them. Chaos ensued as blows were thrown. Attempts to flee were forcibly squelched with batons, but the crew were careful not to break bones. Shattered bones would spoil a subject's blood and waste the food and free passage invested in him by Masterson.

I think that the term the crew used was "crowd control," as if the refugees were rowdy concert-goers needing to be kept from rushing a stage. In truth, it was more like keeping bulls in a pen before the matador slays them. Like the mistreated bulls in a brutal, morally reprehensible sport, the refugees were herded, tortured, and isolated before being led into their watery arena, filled with waves not sand, where they, too, would have their lives extracted from them by those who felt everything from entertainment to a workman's prosaic job satisfaction. The displaced voyagers were no match for what had been assembled to overcome them, and they realized with horrified cognizance that they were now more disposable on the *Grand Rapina* than were even the bullfighting beasts in their own homelands.

Back, back, goes the desire to lure a creature to its death.

Back from the boardrooms, back from the bullrings, back from the Labyrinth of Crete where the Minotaur roamed. The urge to overpower is, perhaps, the oldest one on the planet, and it originated not in our brother the bull but in our enemy the snake. It is the snake who taught man to betray his Lord, himself, and his neighbor.

Survival instincts are difficult to thwart, though. Living beings resist death. Man learned to farm in the thistles outside of Paradise, and the snake learned to crawl in the dust instead of to walk. Those who resisted extermination on the *Grand Rapina* have names, and wherever they are now — I pray in a heaven free from the machinations of hatred — they are still known by their personal names.

Edwardo, from Colon, near the Caribbean, fought back with a bull's strength, but was throttled in the stairwell until he bled from his eyes. This injury made him unsuitable for study, and, therefore, useless, and so he was never seen again, although his two daughters looked for him hour by hour for months. In their grief, one daughter became psychologically mute, and the other developed a taste for the relief of the crimson poppies.

Winsome Sofia, from Belize, was gripped from behind around her waist on the stair landing, and with her long tresses and soft brown eyes, she was appraised by three male crew members as too desirable to be lost in some crazy pool experiment, and so she was pulled through a doorway and into a linen closet, where she was raped by each man as the others kept watch and took videos on their cell phones. Sofia's body was not discovered for weeks, as she was left under a pile of white linen tablecloths that were perfectly woven as her winding sheets. When the cockroaches came, she was found.

Hector, his father's only son, was stabbed with a screw driver.

Gabby was smothered when she spat in the face of her killer.

Amidst their struggles and panicked outcries, the detainees were searched for weapons, stripped naked, unceremoniously hosed down, and forced into the adjacent swimming pool that would be electronically and chemically manipulated to influence their blood chemistry. The pool had been customized cruelly for the purpose, but it groaned under the weight of the many souls pushed into it all at one time. Perhaps the gunite and concrete were weeping at the malfeasance they were forced to commit.

This "swim" was the first step in creating a race-specific vaccine that would be marketed to the world leaders who wished to sterilize this people, so as to rid their nation of those they considered a vermin presence. To these racist leaders, it was a bonus that for their considerable investment in the *Grand Rapina*'s voyage, many of those who were kidnapped would not live through the blood-drawing: Not only would these unfortunates be unable to reproduce in the long-term, they would never end up within a host nation's borders, needing immediate support and resources.

And when the time came for countries to set about administering the sterilizing vaccine in which they'd invested, the malignant leaders knew how to proclaim what a pity it was that the Latin American ethnicity that participated in their benevolent "vitamin drive" was somehow irreparably sterile. The leaders would feign scientific ignorance, plead that they had known nothing at all was amiss, or even say that it was the poor people's fault, and then go home to their palaces to eat pink ice creams in freedom and happiness.

I have not been reading dystopian novels. Like my trial judges, I can scarcely believe Walker Masterson's goals for genocide, and the help that was offered to him by murderous diplomats. From the comfort and grandeur of their penthouses, they wished to reach down to rearrange God's vision of humanity, with a drug that was made from the blood of Latin Americans, many of whom would die immediately from the process of creating it, and who would unknowingly impact even their distant kindred.

The naked crowd of refugees stood exposed and shivering at the pool's edge. The pool was empty of water. Clinging to one another, made to be ashamed, the runaways were prodded into the middle of the vacant space by crew members in swimming trunks. The youngest and strongest runaways were brought in first, with the elderly positioned to form a ring around them. The pool bottom was frigid and sharp against the people's bare feet. Some cut their heels and bled on the decorative, dolphin-shaped tiles.

As the refugees huddled, cold seawater began to trickle in and then aggressively flow from the waterfalls overhead. The water gushed in at a high rate, and soon it was filling the pool quickly. In a few moments, the water had reached a depth of two feet, and swirled around the refugees' calves. Shortly, spouts in the plastic palm trees flooded their artificial branches, and the rocks and boulders that encircled the pool's perimeter dripped with cascading water. The sound of falling water filled the pool's cavernous space.

An engineer watching from cameras in the spa gave a report to Jenny Elihu in the medical center. He was one of the many aloof professionals that I had seen in line when boarding the *Grand Rapina*. "We've started the initial fill. Can I take it from here, Doctor?" he said.

"Go ahead, Bedminster."

The water suddenly increased in force. In moments, the level was above the green glass tiles marking the normal waterline for the children's section, where mosaic whales swam happily in a benign circle. When the water level reached three and a half feet, the refugees lifted their smallest children above their heads, and the screaming began. The people suddenly realized that they were being purposely drowned, and the water roiled with their flailing.

The crew members in trunks pushed the people back with long, spiked poles. Runaways climbing the pool's sides were clubbed. Heads dipped above and below the rising water. Blood was accidentally let, which brought a rebuke from Dr. Elihu. "I need that!" she complained into her microphone. "Don't make them bleed yet!"

It was then that one of the ancient grandmothers lost her footing, and she disappeared with upstretched hands under the roaring blue dyes that were being pumped in as a disinfectant. The purifying agent was needed now, because in their fear, some of the refugees were losing control of their bladders. The grandmother's son swam frantically under the coursing waters, but her drowned body was soon fished out by a crew member, who threw a metal lasso around the old woman's neck. This removal was easy to do because of the foresight of positioning the old within easiest reach. The dead woman, dripping and limp, was covered with a long, plastic sheath and wheeled away on what looked to be the aluminum catering cart from the Sky on Reserve. The son was punched into submission by a worker who jumped into the water.

"Beginning Phase Two," Bedminster said into his microphone. "Our sensors say that their blood pressure is rising, but their anxiety hormones are still within range. The ratios won't affect the optimal oxygen levels for vaccine development. We'll raise the temperature now."

As if a switch had been turned on atop a stove to boil a pot, the water temperature in the pool began to increase. A thin vapor of mist developed over the waters. A few refugees cried out in despair. Weeping filled the ceiling under the opaque roof, and pushing and shoving intensified in the pool. Simultaneously, as the temperature was raised, the water level was also increased. The pool water now stood in churning undulations at five feet deep. The refugees who could swim began to dog paddle in place, but those who could not swim were quickly extinguished and dragged out from the waters by the crew. The dead were stacked in piles like firewood, since there weren't enough carts to haul everyone away now. Someone suggested that the dead be stored on ice in a Styrofoam cooler, like fish. As another crew member passed the dead under his hands, he robbed them of whatever gold crosses, medallions, and medals they wore, intending to pawn the precious metal in the nearest harbor.

"Load the sulphur canisters now," Jenny Elihu announced. "Make sure you have your masks on."

Specialist Bedminster confirmed the doctor's order. Workers in the pool reached for their stockpile of gas masks, protecting themselves. In seconds, the noxious smell floated over the poolside, carrying an irritant designed to raise the appropriate hormones for study of the captives' blood, but without taking their anxiety hormones too high. "We're reaching the upper limit," Bedminster noted.

The refugees began to shout for deliverance from the steaming waters as they choked in the sulphur fumes. God was beseeched by some, cursed by others. Some parents flung their infants out of the pool and onto the surrounding teak and walnut decking, desperately hoping that their chances for survival there would be higher. In the cloud of gas, the parents could not see the crew members gather up the infants with crushed spines and broken necks and whisk them away in native baskets. Where the babies went, who knows? Murdered? Sold on the black market for body parts?

"I don't want to hear their prayers," Jenny complained into her microphone to Bedminster. "Turn on the recordings of the church bells."

The engineer duly fulfilled the order, and the lovely, holy bells crowded out the cries of the people's suffering. Specialist Bedminster flipped a switch to turn off the noise in his own headphones, too. Instantly, the people's prayers were silenced in his ears, yet the engineer was still in touch with Jenny Elihu. Her voice was loud and clear.

"Our instruments are showing several arrhythmias," Bedminster reported. "Looks like we're going to have some heart attacks."

"If they die, too bad. We've still got enough for valid data. Keep going."

"Yes, Doctor," Bedminster responded.

In twelve minutes, at a very precise moment determined by science, Dr. Elihu gave a gruff order. "It's time to draw the blood. Bring the survivors to me."

"Right away. We'll pull them all out."

And so they were removed from the saltwater pool, and herded down to the medical center in a state of shock so profound that they allowed the tourniquets to bruise their arms for a bloodletting intended to wipe out their race. While they swayed in exhaustion, the lifeforce was drained from their bodies by silent, skilled, and efficient teams in surgical masks and rubber gloves, through flexible tubing linked to sturdy, silicone pouches, in a bloodbath undeterred by the refugees' fainting, shrieking, or pleading. This blood was harvested like Masterson's due, and the survivors were heaped into numerous trips of the wide service elevators (not the stairs this time), and they were dumped with a shove out onto the bitter, criminal boards of the Starlight Deck.

Soon after, the swill of the Vasodilator Diet was spooned by "hospitality staff" into communal stainless-steel bowls, which collected the runaways' tears and reflected their terrified faces. The food was rolled onto the deck with jugs of water for the survivors to serve themselves, if they could manage. The people ate and drank and grieved over their clanking steel bowls, like those used for dogs' kennels, and they were left to wander in their delirium in the confining space without any clues to their future, or the fate of the missing.

And the next group of a hundred or so was hosed, drowned, bled, and dumped. Then the pool was drained, doused with chlorine, and covered with netting until time to ensnare again. This went on day after day. I was preaching from hell, which was not made of flames but of seawater. And the refugees kept coming.

Rumor spread quickly on the *Grand Rapina* about what was happening on the lower decks. Hulking Hazel mysteriously replaced Chris Adamos for bringing our food, and I heard her laughingly relay to her compatriots "the mess going on downstairs." Hazel was oblivious about security, not bothering to lock our cabin door as her predecessor had done so religiously. Shortly, she even abandoned serving our meals. Nothing remained to be brought, anyway. In a sense, then, Candy, Emmie, and I were free now to wander the ship.

Freedom was an illusion, however. Candace told me that in my sleep I begged the Lord to draw a black curtain over my mind to block out my recollections. With the atrocities taking place on the *Grand Rapina*, which would occur many, many times, I could not bear to recall Hazel's cynical laugh, or the faces of those who came to me in the chapel. My psyche remained in chains, even though my body moved about onboard with no oppressor even caring anymore.

Reverting to type, I suppose, I took to meditating on ancient prayers for strength. I grant that some men would have spent their time trying to master the technologies on the ship to communicate with the shore, and others would have plotted a mutinous rebellion. Some men would have drained the liquor shelves in the bars to kill the pain of their confinement. Many men would have been unable to cope altogether. I had my own emergency reaction. I recited from Saint Augustine of Hippo:

> O Lord my God, I believe in you, Father, Son, and Holy Spirit. Insofar as I can, insofar as you have given me the power, I have sought you. I became weary and I labored. O Lord my God, my sole hope, help me to believe and never to cease seeking you. Grant that I may always and ardently seek out your countenance. Give me the strength to seek you, for you help me to find you, and you have more and more given me the hope of finding you. Here I am before you with my firmness and my infirmity. Preserve the first and heal the second.

As I wandered the ship in my depression, I came across a band of refugees who had cleverly strung a fishing line about thirty feet down, out of an unobtrusive window on the Starlight Deck, and were thus feeding themselves. They ate, raw, anything that wriggled out of the sea? No, they had their ancient techniques, their own old ways of surviving, to which they turned. I saw that the people were drying the fish in the scorching sun to cook it, just as their Inca ancestors had done. I wondered how long it would take before Jenny Elihu found out, and what she would do. Would she be able to tell by the runaways' blood work that they had eaten not of the Vasodilator Diet?

Fascinated, I saw that the runaways had just pulled a small octopus from the ocean. Subdued jubilation spread throughout the group, since the fish was snagged in a hefty clump of lustrous seaweed, which is very nutritious. The tangled mass was quickly extracted from the line by men who had clearly done this before, with the octopus separated from its coating of ocean weeds, which were flung into a waiting bucket and kept moist. The pink octopus tentacles were hung, writhing, over a rope that someone had strung like a clothesline in a bright, hot corner. I have to admit that my craw rose when I saw that the octopus had joined a seagull, newly plucked.

I left the Starlight Deck before bringing attention to the "fishing crew."

In their kindness, those refugees sneaked to me three dried bonitos wrapped in a bandana, and gifted in a Panama hat to keep me cool. Touched, I found this gift of food a parallel to the story of loaves and fishes in the Bible. As did the people in that story, I would have to trust that the Lord would provide more than enough. The refugees even insisted that I bless the hat. The true miracle was that they had managed to pull up fish, unseen, while the *Grand Rapina* coursed at between ten and fifteen knots. Some among the refugees had supernatural, fisherman-apostle genes? No, they were feeling the rush of their Inca blood, as descendants of a race storied for its ability to survive food shortages.

The nourishment I gave to Candace and Emmie.

As for me, I was too upset to eat.

* * *

"What's up with that maniac over in the jail? He's raving," said one of the blood takers. The phlebotomist walked around in his comfy clogs, casually filing his fingernails while the custodian mopped the spa floor. "How do you stand it?"

"Jones is losing his grip. I called the chaplain. He's on his way down."

"Why'd you send for him? What's he going to do?"

"Who else would come?"

"Are ye drunk on seaweed and squid ink? How dare ye put the master of the vessel in the brig! I'll be drawing and quartering ye at dawn!"

"I wish he'd shut that up. Dr. Elihu is going to have to do something."

"He's been like that since Amador. You know, that was the first draw. I guess you do know, right? You helped."

"A lot of them croaked. I saw the bodies."

"Well, what can you do?" The custodian wrung his mop in his bucket, feeling philosophical. "Progress isn't pretty. Don't step on my wet tiles."

The two workers watched as Pastor Atterley entered the staircase that led to the jail. His face was tense, his hands clutching his Bible. The pastor was accompanied by a security officer, who was rail thin and light on his feet. The guard was already carefully formulating a plan for how this crisis might end. He liked to nip things in the bud. He had not been recently promoted for nothing.

The caged abuser began to cry for his mother. He had helped to fill the pool, and now was driven mad by what he'd seen. "I didn't know it was going to be like that! It was just a bath! Please don't tell! Please don't tell on me! I didn't know!" Kevin Jones agitatedly paced the four corners of his padded cell, beating his chest. "I was just doing my job! I thought it was going to be a bath!" The young man whimpered and pushed his anguished face into his sleeve.

"All right, all right, that's enough!" Officer Cramer yelled. "I brought you down here to get you out of the way, and you're making trouble for me again!"

The blood taker listened intently. "They're getting him off this ship, and pronto. Wait and see."

The custodian continued to mop. He pushed a folding chair aside to wipe blood off some table legs. Without looking up, "I'm not so sure. He knows too much."

Jones now began to howl like a coyote. The custodian and the phlebotomist could hear Pastor Atterley attempting to calm him. "Kevin, Kevin, let me come inside and we'll talk, we'll talk, Kevin."

"I want my mother, please call my mother!"

"You're not going to need her!"

119

Suddenly, the pastor screamed, "No, no!"

A gunshot cracked like a firework.

The phlebotomist dropped his nail file, startled.

"Hmm. Small caliber," said the custodian. "Not too much to mop up. That's good for me."

The *Grand Rapina*'s brig was thereafter quiet.

On the main deck, the noise of a hovering bird filled the silence.

CHAPTER NINE

Several days passed. The *Grand Rapina* hid in the ocean, doing the Devil's work. The place and the time blended together in the vastness of the South American water, and both seemed without boundaries, almost to the point of absorbing me. I fought to remain separate, emotionally, from the waves and the hours, for the ancient Pacific Ocean had a way of luring me into a desire to meld with it, to dissolve into it, to permanently join it in its rhythms.

Overhead, I could hear small aircraft, presumably on the way from Quito, Ecuador, near Manta, to the Galapagos Archipelago. People who were not prisoners were on their way to island hop. Those full-time locals who worked on the inhospitable, volcanic islands would make them feel amenable, entertaining the giddy tourists and educating the circumspect scientists drawn to the Enchanted Islands. It filled me with agony to listen to the sounds of airborne freedom, to the calls of mechanical birds in the skies, knowing that, for me, they were unreachable.

My mind turned to the life of a fellow spiritual sojourner known for his time exploring this area, a recollection that tormented me. How different and unbounded was his experience!

I think that Charles Darwin and I would have begun by comparing our long, gray beards.

Every relationship needs an early ice breaker. From his nineteenth century portraits, I can tell that his beard was a bit straggly. I used to keep mine well-kempt and trimmed. Neither of us made any attempt to hide the faded brown color imbued by our years.

From beards, I think that we would have moved on to discussing our common travel destinations, for he went over to the Galapagos to see the finches, and I listened, albeit involuntarily, to my own kind of birds just off of those same islands. I never got to see the finches or the famous blue-footed boobies or any of the Galapagos birds close up, and that was a loss to me, given that I sailed so near to their exotic homeland. Darwin, on the other hand, saw the birds in person and studied them so closely that his observations impacted the interpretation of scientific (and theological) thought forever. How we've evolved in our thinking!

From beards and birds, I think that we would have moved on to our mutual education as parsons, both of us acknowledging humbly that we never really understand what God is about in his world, but we are dazzled by its beauty, variety, and mystery. Together, Darwin and I might also have pondered the world's destiny. There, our paths might have diverged. I like to think that we would have ultimately arrived at the same place, though, with me taking the spiritual turnpike to the right and him taking the intellectual avenue to the left. I like to think that the good Lord saw us both coming from afar, and went out to stand in the roads of heaven to watch for both prodigals coming home to him, just by different routes.

Funny, I write about myself in the past tense.

One day without explanation, I was barred from the Starlight Deck on the *Grand Rapina* and was only able to see the refugees in the chapel from that point on. I was alarmed by this development. Still being an innocent, myself, I internalized that the separation was somehow my fault, and that the runaways were being protected from me. Faulting myself was absurd. Only the conscientious blame themselves. Crew members were posted as guards on the deck, carrying semi-automatic weapons that I'd never come across in Glenville. I wouldn't have even known how to hold such a gun in my hands. And how many of those hideous instruments of death were onboard?

To pass the time on the ship, I began to study the constellations with guides from the little ship's library. The stars in their twinkling formations dazzled me at night, and attempting to recognize the animals and other shapes outlined by the peoples of old was an effort that fascinated me, though I confess that I could seldom tell the scorpion in the sky from the dog. How astonishing it was, so close to the equator, to see stars in both the Northern and Southern Hemispheres!

Except for entering the Starlight Deck and the bridge, I wandered the vessel.

I found where the crew's secret disco and bar were tucked away, after accidentally wandering in. It was Sodom and Gomorrah on the ocean, from a pastor's point of view. Many ship workers who were married onshore did not consider themselves legally matched at sea, judging from the inebriated embraces in slinky get-ups by people who took off nearly everything except their incriminating wedding rings. How prudish of me to notice. These adulterous half-dressed took time out from their assignations to share that we were on the way to the Port of Callao, in Peru, a natural harbor first frequented by Francisco Pizarro, mainly to rob the Incas. Our food supply onboard was depleted, but there was plenty of sex and booze, apparently.

"Why are we headed to Callao?" I asked. "What's there for the *Grand Rapina*?"

"Moze Balodis has the itch up his nose," a drunk sniffed. "It's got more crack than anyplace else in the world!"

"He's meeting his wife at the airport!" a group in a corner booth laughed.

"More poor people to leech!" a dishwasher sneered. "We're running low!"

I left the bar quickly, before I was propositioned.

By walking around, I learned where thousands of pounds of vegetables were cooled, when we had them. I found a movie theater, a kennel for pets, a gym with an adjacent, cavernous space for a rock-climbing wall and a zipline. Expensive artwork was for sale at one time in the *Grand Rapina*'s past, and oil paintings were still hanging in a gallery. I came across the accoutrements for wine tastings, cookie-baking contests, and private culinary instructions; all of this, and much more, had been offered before the cruise ship went rogue.

I discovered many odd and interesting things, such as that most of the walls on the cruise liner were magnetized for holding schedules and calendars and the like, and that the doors leading to the prow on the main deck were hidden, to discourage guests from having private disaster-movie moments that could lead to midnight falls off the ship. I was seldom questioned by the crew about where I was going, and came to believe that the general discipline and professional protocols on the *Grand Rapina* were disintegrating into nothingness.

The anxiety from the dissolution of order took a toll. I began to meditate, for if I could not leave the ship in my body, I could leave the *Grand Rapina* in my mind. I went inside myself and reached out to the Lord from there. I strolled the promenade and contemplated these words from the 23rd Psalm:

> Even though I walk through the valley of the shadow of death,
> I will fear no evil, for you are with me.
> Your rod and your staff,
> they comfort me.

And these from Isaiah 43:

> When you pass through the waters, I will be with you,
> and through the rivers, they will not overflow you.
> When you walk through the fire, you will not be burned,
> and flame will not scorch you.
> For I am YAHWEH your God,
> the Holy One of Israel,
> your Savior.

It was through meditation that I found I was able to cope. My surroundings, which were nothing more than luxurious confinement, would recede out of my awareness and be replaced by my mental focus, which was a total concentration on knowing that the Lord God was not at all a prisoner at sea, as I was. He was free, moving at large in the Spirit, and aware of the pressing needs of all those who were suffering on the *Grand Rapina*. If only he had chosen to lift me up and away, physically; still, I became calmer for periods of time when he lifted me up, spiritually, in meditation, and for those short respites from emotional duress I was grateful.

My long-dormant desire to write re-emerged. When it had waned, at least for the writing of scholarly pieces, I had interpreted that lack of desire as a sign that I should retire from full-time ministry. Now, in the face of a different kind of pastoral duty, I was surprised that my inner spiritual person emerged in writing as in my younger days. I began to see images in my mind. I began to think in narratives of prose. I even began to tell myself little short stories.

There once was a farmer boy far from home, far away from any land that he had ever plowed. He was on the sea, and no furrows there would keep their shape, nor remain deep, nor remain neat. The farmer boy knew that he had none of the right kind of seeds. He determined that he would plant pearls.

The first time that a helicopter whisked away with the blood that had been drawn, I had the strangest sensation, the feeling that I was watching souls ascend into the universe, tethered to the tail of the aircraft. I was on the main deck. It was mid-afternoon on a cloudy day, with the dome of round sky overhead seemingly lined with gray-blue slate stones. I almost worried that these stones would detach from the dome and tumble down in sharp shards all over my body, such was my state of mind. Every hour, I felt that I was being stoned to death one rock at a time, and if they should all tumble out of the ether at once in a salvo of projectiles, so much the better for quickly ending my emotional turmoil. So I stopped worrying and instead let a welcome of rocks register in me. God's will be done.

I didn't know it, but I had wandered onto a helipad, which was concealed by every type of cruise ship junk, from vinyl deck chairs and assorted inflatable beach balls, yoga mats, a couple of barbecue grills, to the steel drums and keyboards played by the Jamaican band that performed whenever the *Grand Rapina* wasn't busy capturing runaways. A storm was building at sea as we made our way to the Port of Callao, near Lima, and the cruise ship began to pitch and roll, becoming a moving target for a helicopter fast approaching through the clouds in the distance. It came at the *Grand Rapina* like an apparition, its outline indistinct in the air at first, but gradually acquiring definition.

No one in the ship's crew materialized to shoo me away, so I moved to the nearby pub lounge to discreetly watch from a window as the pilot considered how to proceed in the shifting winds above a cruise ship bobbing like a bathtub toy. Obviously, no one had planned for his landing, because of the junky debris on the deck. He seemed determined to try, however, flying into the wind off the bow. The pilot came low, within a hundred yards of the deck, rotors spinning and roaring, then was swept up and away by the gusts. He flew close again, seemed almost to teeter, and was swept away by the wind once more. What would he do?

Somewhere along the line in my weeks on the ship, I had developed sea legs, and the whole spectacle with the helicopter unfolded above me without my stomach bouncing into my throat at all. Candace, with her cast iron innards, would have been so proud of me, but it could have been that my stomach, like my morale, could barely summon the will needed to respond to the situation. I found the noise from the helicopter's whirring rotors, as well as the howl from a hysterical, banshee wind, more discomfiting than the ship's roll, but I refused to be driven away from the scene by the racket. I had to know what was about to happen.

I struggled to consider a criminal's point of view. Of course! It had never occurred to me before that the vials and pouches of blood could not stay indefinitely onboard, and that they must be spirited away to a much larger lab, or spoil in the tropical heat. The ship's refrigeration would not suffice for long. The helicopter's arrival was the dramatic solution. Out of port, it must have posed as a medevac unit.

I realized a few minutes into his tumultuous hover that the pilot was not attempting to land on the *Grand Rapina*. It was too risky in the rising swells, for the ship was unstable. He was trying to come as close as he could. I could see the pilot speaking into his headset, leaning forward to get a good look at the deck. The superstructure was wholly in front of him, but visibility was deteriorating. The pilot must have been in constant touch with Dr. Elihu, deliberating, calculating the risk of collision.

Suddenly, two broad doors on the helicopter jerked open to reveal a wide interior bay, and a winch began to unfurl as the aircraft was buffeted around in the mist. In a moment of insight, I realized that if the helicopter could not go to the blood, then the blood would go to the helicopter. A sizable metal basket on a cable, guided by a winchman, was lowered down out of the aircraft, moving slowly toward the deck, and the basket seemed weighted to withstand the swirling winds. It did not rapidly twist or wind itself up in the air, but came straight down, alighted on the deck, and then, as if a signal had been given, the world exploded with frantic activity.

The *Grand Rapina*'s crew formed the line of a bucket brigade, and hand-over-hand, they loaded the metal carrier with insulated cardboard boxes that contained the blood that had been drawn from the refugees. Fighting the wind, half a dozen passes were made by the *Grand Rapina*'s workers before the helicopter pilot was satisfied, or else was instructed by Jenny Elihu to leave. The winchman leaned out of the bay, watched as the crew members secured the last box of blood, and hauled the metal basket up and inside. He then checked his cords and gear, waved with some flair, and roughly pushed both the helicopter's doors shut. The pilot immediately sped away, with tail lights strobing and flashing in the gloom.

And I saw a hundred souls flying behind him, holding hands in the air. Their ethereal selves streamed behind the cases of their blood, reluctant to separate from the life force that had once sustained them. I stared into the gathering clouds, and watched the souls glide far away, and prayed that before the helicopter landed, they would be released from the invisible chains that bound them to the vehicle. Otherwise, where were they to go?

As for me, I had to get back to my suite.

In the process, I was nearly mown down by the card tables, end tables, dining tables, lamps, chairs, dishes, cutlery, glasses, coffee pots, and flower arrangements that were flying everywhere now. Whole meters of tablecloths fell off, dragging salt and pepper shakers, napkins, candles, and menus with them. The chandeliers swayed. I could not stand upright any longer, yet I had to hazard taking the elevator, knowing that I'd be tossed like a rag doll in the stairways.

When I made it to the stainless-steel elevator doors, I was dumbstruck as a coating of icy seawater started to sheet them, reflecting my face in wavy distortion. I got inside, anyway. I could feel the floor of the elevator vibrating and rumbling uncertainly as I rode up. The overhead lighting dimmed. Just as I stepped out, the electrical power shut down. One door never opened completely, and I pushed it aside, wet as it was. Ten more seconds in the elevator and I would have been trapped. I stepped onto a landing and got my bearings. I turned right and walked nearly at a run.

As I rushed to my cabin, the ship lurched, throwing me hard against a wall. I wasn't knocked out. I went on. I came around a corner and nearly collided with two nameless workers who were swiping the carpets with long squeegee poles, sweeping the water up. I slowed my pace, with my feet pushed up against the wall's baseboards, and my shoulders leaning in exactly the opposite direction. At this uncomfortable angle, I made my way down the corridor to my stateroom.

I yelled for my wife while still down the hallway. When Candace opened the door, I saw a forty-foot swell crashing over our balcony. The sea was leaping into my private world, throwing itself around in foamy insistence. It rose up in a fearsome gray wall, topped with a white frilly fringe, opened wide in a wet embrace, spread itself thin, then retreated. It seemed to be thinking of how to invade me, like an intelligent animal wanting inside, one relentless, one who knew its own strength. The ocean refused to give up, just kept leaping and frothing and battering.

My wife and Emmie were pale with fear, and for the first time I sincerely hoped that Captain Moze Balodis knew what he was doing. Why had he not taken us farther out to sea, to go around this storm? It was the helicopter! He had to stay in the helicopter's fuel range, and now we were stuck. As I watched another wave crash over our terrace, the ship shuddered violently, and our television detached from the wall and smashed into a million pieces.

When we knelt to pick up the brittle glass and plastic, lest we stumble in it, there came a loud pounding on our stateroom door. I answered it with a whip of TV cord in my hand, a weapon if I needed it. Hazel stood in the hallway, gripping the doorjamb with her big knuckles to keep from being tossed in the storm. "Officer Vera says you come downstairs," she said sternly, "the people are scared."

I looked back to judge the reactions of Candace and Emmie. My wife spoke for both. "You're not leaving us here. We're coming, too!"

"It's twenty flights, and there's no power!"

"The crew elevator's on the backup generator. Come down with me," Hazel commanded.

When we arrived at the Starlight Deck, we saw that the guards had abandoned their post. My family stepped out into a world that we'd never seen before. It was like a dying village. What did Vera expect me to do? Hazel did not bother to look, and she vanished away as the elevator closed, to try to wait out the gale.

Not all of the runaways had fared as well as those who knew how to fish. Many on the Starlight Deck looked as if they'd not been fed in days. Refugees had still continued to come to my chapel services, where I could get a look at them, but not all of them, it was clear. Some, those who suffered the most, had not left the deck in many days, and I'd not been aware of their physical straits. Had they not been given even the

Vasodilator Diet after their blood drawing? This devastation was what Captain Balodis and Dr. Elihu had not wanted me to see.

I walked among the crowds, aghast. People were ashen, barely alive. I turned to Emmie. "Ask him when was the last time he ate. And her. Ask her."

"Five days ago we were given clam shells and fish heads in water," the man whispered in Spanish. The woman nodded weakly.

These people were starving! Even the Vasodilator Diet was being withheld. Dr. Elihu was killing the people after she was done with bleeding them!

As I walked about, an old Honduran couple approached me. "Father, please, we want to be married before we die," Emmie translated. "We have been together for forty years and have three living children, but we have never been married in the eyes of God. Please, Father, we want to be married before we die."

"Emmie, explain that I'm not a priest." I shook my head, No.

The old couple listened. "But are you not a man of God?"

"Yes, but it can't be the time or place, can it?" I said.

"Please, marry us while there is time."

"You could give them your blessing, James," Candy offered gently. "It would be enough, at least for now."

I placed the old couple's hands atop each other and made the sign of the cross on their aged brows. "What therefore God has joined together, don't let man tear apart," I improvised. The old woman turned to her mate and smiled softly.

My heart nearly broke in my chest at these sights.

I burst out of the Starlight Deck, leapt down a short flight of stairs, and ran past the crew laundry. I had to see the extent of the loss. I had to face something that I swore I'd always avoid, me, a pastor, one acquainted with death.

I went to the morgue.

I barged inside and took over the space. Two off-duty men in casual sweats looked up. I sensed that they were hiding from something, maybe avoiding orders from the Captain?

"Get out of here, you're not allowed in here!" a crew member said, pushing back his chair to throw me out. His co-worker stood to offer support.

I ignored them and kept running. A spirit of rage possessed me as I lost control of myself, rushing from mortuary cabinet to mortuary cabinet in search of the bodies. An unlocked shelf, nothing there, an unlocked shelf, nothing there. It was just as I thought. Incalculable carnage! The morgue was empty!

I ran to the man in the weight-lifting shirt and grabbed him around his neck. I shook him with all of my power. "Where are they, where are they?" I growled. "It must be scores!"

The man was shocked at my strength, pulling at my wrists. An old man was squeezing the life out of him. "They go over the side at night," he whispered, choking, "we push them overboard at night!"

"Alive?"

"Sometimes! So what!"

"Don't tell him that! Don't confess, are you crazy?"

As the co-worker moved to pull me away, I let go of the sputtering man. The two began to argue, shoving each other, and yelling.

"You are *so stupid*, what have you done!"

"He got me by the neck, why didn't you *help*?"

I left the morgue in a high state of fury.

I returned to the Starlight Deck.

The storm had intensified, and Candy and Emmie were clinging to one another and to strangers. As I walked among the people, barely able to keep my footing, I was horrified at what I was seeing and hearing. How long had this been going on?

First, some of the children came to me in tears, pleading for me to take away the "red-headed bear who would put them in cages." Someone had started a tale of a fierce creature with red fur that would kidnap them and take them away from their parents. Had the crew started the myth to try to keep the children in check? It was not enough to starve them? Who would do such a thing? Even above the storm's danger, the children feared being caged.

Worse, as I walked, I found the despicable signs of voodoo everywhere. Satan was running amok. Goddesses were being implored. The nominally Catholic had reverted to pagan ways, having brought those practices with them. I saw no protective medallions, no rosary beads. I was not a priest, but I recalled an ancient prayer of exorcism, and recited it to myself. I'd learned it as an academic exercise in seminary ages ago, but now I needed the full power of its eviction, to try to rid the Starlight Deck of what had permeated it through unclean practices.

The pagan horrors the people tried to hide as I walked among them, but I used whatever authority I had to demand that the primitive trappings, black magic tools, hallucinogenics like peyote cactus crowns, and everything else vile, be destroyed at once. The articles disappeared from view, yes, but I knew that the old rituals remained. They'd endured for thousands of years, and I was trying to abolish them in the middle of a gale, from people who clung to them as they realized they were slowly being sacrificed themselves. I felt my inadequacy as a pastor, and while I knew that the pagan ways were entrenched, I worried that for many onboard Christianity was, at best, only a respectable veneer of spiritual coating over other primitive beliefs that the people more earnestly turned to in a crisis.

Were my services as a chaplain completely unnecessary, then? What a mistake Majestic Waves had made in even hiring me, potentially. The company assumed that the refugees were more Christian than they really were, and that they could be controlled by a Christian authority figure. If the people did not turn to the love and protection of Jesus in the worst hours of their lives, did they see me as a failed shaman? I couldn't address these questions, neither answer them nor refute them, but I knew what was in my own heart: I had been called by the Lord to offer spiritual help on this evil vessel. Whether or not my help was accepted was outside of my control.

And then the *Grand Rapina* groaned with an unearthly, ominous creak, listed to port nearly fifty degrees, and went still. An engine had failed. The ship turned on her beam ends, defenseless. I feared for the hull, if we should be driven to a rocky coast in the blinding rain. Every deck on the ship went black. Inside the winds, there were shouts and screams. Water rushed underfoot, swirling, rising, coming through the walls, down the stairs, over the railings, onto the Starlight Deck. Suddenly, there was silence among the people, who waited to die in the grip of the howling waves.

I fell to my knees.

Seawater poured over my khakis, drenching me up to the waist.

I thought I was going to drown.

In my mind, I imagined that Candace would place a blanket over a trembling child.

Emmie sat shivering, her wet hair dripping down her back.

No. No. No.

It was fear, only fear.

No more fainting.

I will tell my judges I tried to be brave.

* * *

Hazel stomped in from the Starlight Deck to finish her chore. She felt singled out and put upon. She stuffed First Officer Vera's belongings into a duffel bag, as she'd been ordered by him to do. Tony Vera didn't expect her loyalty, he wanted only compliance, which came with a strain of treachery, unbeknownst to him.

"Do I get anything out of this, uh, No, I do not," Hazel complained to herself. "He's got his nerve, he thinks I won't tell," the big woman huffed, yanking a zipper on the duffel. "He just thinks he's going to sneak right out when that 'copter comes back. He just thinks he's getting away, not a care in the world!"

Hazel rifled through the officer's things in his quarters. Under the threat of punishing her, he could make her do his bidding, but she was not obligated to be courteous about it. Hazel paused to look at a photo in a silver frame on Tony Vera's desk. It was lightweight, only plated silver, not sterling, not worth stealing to sell. She opened his closet and ran her meaty hands over his fancy uniforms. Could they be pawned — but where would she store them? Would anybody buy his hats online? She opened a trinket case in his dresser. Cuff links. Those went into her pocket. The jeweler in port would tell her if they were fake gold.

"Do you think five hundred dollars would've broke him? No, I do not," Hazel continued. "I'm glad I showed that pastor what's really going on. Vera's going to jail! That chaplain will treat me better."

Hazel picked up a silk kimono from off of the officer's double bed. The robe was feminine and printed with a lovely lotus. The worker held it under her nose to smell the fabric's perfume. She pushed her arm through a sleeve to see if it would fit. "And I bet I know who this belongs to. Hazel needs to get paid for what she knows. I know it all! Doctor Elihu, guess what, your boyfriend's leaving you!"

As Hazel snooped and packed, the lights went out all around. She clenched her jaw, frightened. "What's that, the storm, what happened?" The *Grand Rapina* quaked and groaned in the swells. Hazel felt the ship tip sharply onto its left side, nearly completely over. Loose possessions in Officer Vera's rooms tumbled into a heap, curtains rods fell, the glass in the windows strained under the pressure. Hazel reached out in the dark to grab the bed, which was bolted down tight to the floor. Terrified, she thought that the ship might capsize, and she began to scream. "Help, Tony Vera, take me with you! Somebody, take me, too! I don't want to drown on this boat!"

The demon of the Pacific, the false god worshipped on the Starlight Deck with the voodoo beads, was listening and was with Hazel. He stood in for the fleeing First Officer. Smirking, the fallen angel granted Hazel's wish.

When the curtain pole went flying into her chest, spearing its decorative brass coils all the way through her big bosoms and out the other side, Hazel was shocked for a moment that she did not feel water eating her up, and that the bedspread was still dry in her hands.

Then she bled out all over the silk kimono.

CHAPTER TEN

The winds blew as if barreling from the tunnels of hell, but we were not sinking. With the ship tossing in the ocean, rising and falling thunderously, excess pressure had built in the pipes to crack the weak places. The *Grand Rapina* had busted a water main on the Starlight Deck, and the din of the rushing water indoors competed with the roar of the winds outside. I was disoriented and could not rely on my sense of hearing to gauge the danger.

Although water furiously gushed all around me, pouring down walls, draining from ceilings, lifting carpet and tiles as I unsteadily tried to walk on them, even escaping in bubbly gurgles through the light sockets, I was not losing my mind, and, most significantly, we were not taking on saltwater. Crew members scrambled to repair the main, and then they pumped out the standing water, doing this strenuous work with the storm making their every move more difficult. Though the wind sounded frightful, and the water coursing everywhere was unnerving, they were not so much to be feared as the waves, particularly a rogue one.

We were structurally buoyant for the time being, as far as I could tell, with the snap and buzz of the redundant power systems restoring the fin stabilizers, which soon corrected most of the *Grand Rapina*'s listing side roll. The ballast tanks, holding water full of fleas and cholera like on most ships, were also working to balance us. It was a relief to walk upright again, not at some uncomfortable angle. We were still pitching, front to back, however, and having lost an engine, we were tossed every which way in the Pacific off of the Galapagos Islands. The *Grand Rapina*'s bow was resolutely facing into the crashing waves, but we could not keep a course.

Captain Balodis, typically so silent, gave an update on the broadcast system, which I could barely hear. His timing was questionable, like his judgement. As if anybody cared in the throes of the weather, when the keel coming apart from the ship seemed not entirely out of the question, Moze described in excruciating detail the meteorological causes of this storm.

"We have encountered a sub-tropical storm that is transitioning into a tropical event, with a storm center that is warm, close thunderstorms, and a broad and evenly dispersed wind field that is presently turning in a clockwise direction," the Captain explained with an accent like a Baltic weatherman. Horrified passengers wanted only to know when it all would cease. The Captain admitted that the situation was worse than he'd expected, particularly on the western side of South America, which was not often prone to these types of stormy incidents.

As if trying to restore his credibility and distance himself from fault, Moze went on to blame malfunctioning satellites, the ineptitude of South American meteorologists, Poseidon, his poor digestion, and all the tea in China. In closing, he guessed how long it would be before we made it through the gale, provided that the ship held together. It was a fine time to display his doubtful expertise. "We are going to ride through this storm. I estimate twenty-four hours will suffice." And that was it. Captain Balodis resumed his characteristic silence. His words once again became rare and watertight.

I wanted to punch Moze in the face. I'm not certain who he was trying to educate — the crew, I guess, not the refugees or myself — but regardless of the poorly timed delivery of the insights from the Captain, it would be nearly another thirty-six hours until we came out on the other side of the gale, and in that period, I died thirty-six times. Every hour, I was petrified, as were Candy and Emmie.

This fear spread throughout the ship like ink squirted from an octopus. It went everywhere, indelibly. After two days of agonizing terror on the swirling ocean, the *Grand Rapina*'s crew had had enough. I heard mutinous rumbles among them. Too much was being asked of them, they whispered, from keeping total secrecy about the ship's macabre mission to enduring a life-threatening gale that Moze Balodis could have avoided, if he'd been a better Captain. Like the skies overhead, the ship's atmosphere was dark and sparking with electric tension.

It is a very dangerous state of affairs when a crew loses its confidence in its Master while on a voyage. The crew began to actively search amongst its own ranks for a new leader, even considering those who ordinarily mopped the floors, to find a seaman who might guide the mighty ocean liner, old school-style and by the stars, since Captain Balodis and his staff with all of their automated technology and formal training seemed to be failing in their charge. The panic was palpable and rising. There was no talk of where to sail, just of who should take over. The crew thought of how to commandeer, but not about how to authentically command. This is the usurper's perennial shortsightedness.

Though there was more than one engine on the *Grand Rapina*, the most seasoned workers knew that without all six diesel engines fully functioning, the Captain would never be able to make it to the Port of Callao, Peru, especially in a storm. Propulsion would be inadequate, among a hundred other problems. Wherever Moze was going, he was going to have to limp there, and the days of self-sufficiently hiding at sea were over. There was no plan. There was not enough to eat. Rumors erupted like hot lava. Among the common crew, the hidden things began to manifest, like repressed anger, roiling resentment, and gathering rebellion.

And plentiful guns.

Certain of the workers knew very well that what looked like an orange and smelled of citrus is not always an orange. In those Masterson crates had come, under the fragrant fruit, stockpiles of hundreds of semi-automatic weapons, in various states of assembly. The workers broke these out and paraded with them boldly, and thus I discovered one of the reasons why we had so little food anymore: The crates that had been loaded onto the *Grand Rapina* at so many ports contained more firearms than fruit and vegetables. Mr. Masterson had a side venture: arms dealer, with the occasional stolen pre-Columbian artifact thrown in to decorate his coffee table.

When the gale broke at last, it left another tempest in its place.

The crew seized the ship on a Sunday morning, with crackling gunfire and hysterical shouting, with men and women putting down their wrenches and stock pots and dust rags, and crawling from the crannies everywhere on the *Grand Rapina*, incensed, indignant. As they ran amok in their fervor, with workers from almost every nation, initially I didn't know whether to run to their aid or hide from them. There was not an officer's epaulette in sight. I found myself in the middle of an insurrection, and my only survival strategy was the instinctual impulse to stay out of the way.

No one asked for my help to seize the ship, and yet, no one shot me in the forehead as I refrained from participating in taking it over. Incredibly, as events took place, I was allowed to witness the takeover as if I were a disinterested bystander, as someone with no stake, definitely as an outsider. I wandered unconstrained up and down the decks at will. I have sometimes wondered if my guardian angel had given me temporary physical invisibility, but it is more likely that the mutineers found me essentially ineffectual, non-threatening, and ignored me.

Shortly, judging by the emphases the fevered crew displayed, like disabling the officers' chain of command, I learned that the mutinous crew had no intention of freeing the refugees, although the workers had no idea what to do with them, either. The crew assumed the runaways were my problem, as were the vials of their blood. Perhaps this was the reason that I had been preserved in the ship's takeover: I of all aboard had spent the most time with the refugees, had been hired to provide for their spiritual care, and if anybody were to consider their lives and safety at all, it would have to be me, by default. So unconcerned with the refugees were the mutineers, the takeover did not even impact the Starlight Deck, where the revolting workers seemed to think that only useless human cargo was stored.

As the vessel's authority structures shifted before my eyes, I accepted the role of guardian, feeling that I had simply gone from protecting the refugees from one terrible master to a different one. I suspected that if there were complications with the runaways — anything that might annoy or inconvenience a vindictive dishwasher, for one, or a menacing bar keep — the working classes would take notice of the helpless runaways and wreak vengeance on them, not caring anymore about the value of their blood. I sensed that, given the mutineers' increasing volatility, the refugees would be extinguished like mere flies that are swatted, out of enraged pique or a desire to destroy evidence of the *Grand Rapina*'s sins. There would be no more attempts to keep them even nominally alive in order to harvest their blood. My mission expanded to prevent this annihilation.

As for the ship's original goal — extracting the blood for lethal vaccines — to my knowledge, astoundingly, it was never mentioned again, and its creator and supervisor, Dr. Jenny Elihu, did not come forth to claim it. She hid like a coward in the burgundy-leather shadows of the smokers' lounge, among the leftover tobacco-leaf fumes sucked from Cuban cigars. How justified it would have been for the murderous student of healthcare to contract emphysema. Jenny was a traitorous doctor, even though her surname evoked an honorable family heritage of closeness to God, the Great Physician. She would never presume to play God again.

Blood drawing was something from the distant past, something that the professional overlords had wanted, and now the revised goal was to sail the *Grand Rapina* to wherever the crew could establish their own New World. The whole focus of the cruise ship changed, with the crew in favor of getting the damaged vessel to a safe haven, to any haven that would have them, where presumably their plans for their future would coalesce.

I took this undisciplined retrenchment to mean that the mutinous workers had never found their new leader, for no one emerged among the crew with the foresight to envision what would happen when they came into a port, loaded as the ship was with bloody vials, bloody victims, and guns. They had no new Captain, as it were. The mutineers lived by surviving in the moment, expressing their displeasure at their situation, and experiencing the thrill of power. They were consumed with unreservedly expressing their outrage and angst, yet not a thought was given as to how to construct the revamped social order they lusted for.

The result was animalistic mob behavior, like that seen in the wilds of the bird kingdom, when prey species as a group swamp a predator to overcome an imminent threat. Similarly, the *Grand Rapina*'s crew thought themselves the prey and the staff, their predators; the crew were angrily determined to upturn this order and tear their abusers to pieces. I intended to keep the refugees from the carnage. In some circumstances, I might have even been able to empathize with how the crew members saw themselves as almost as abused as the runaways held captive on the Starlight Deck, but when their actions devolved into mob violence, they lost whatever small sense of compassion I might have been able to feel for them.

I heard through the bubbling rumors that Moze Balodis had been confined to his quarters and was not taking it well. His elegant superiority, which had shown itself to be superficial, was literally tied up.

I admit that I smirked at this news. Let him join the club. I had no pastoral impulse to go to visit him in his distraught situation, even if the crew had allowed me to make an appeal for his release. Privately, in my heart, I was glad that he had been deposed. He was not a man who could be trusted with authority, in my opinion. The other professional staff and officers did what they were told by the crew, at gunpoint.

Meanwhile, the *Grand Rapina* was adrift, whether by design, purposely without anchoring, I did not know. What was First Officer Vera thinking? Was he in command of the vessel? If not, who was in charge? We were hundreds of miles off the coast of Ecuador, drifting below the Galapagos Archipelago in a vast portion of the Pacific without any guidance.

Though authority and control were upside down all around them, for the runaways on the Starlight Deck nothing had changed. A spirit of captivity still ran unchecked. Starvation still stalked among the refugees. I was hungry, too, as were Candace and Emmie. Fishing off the side of the ship had been out of the question in the gale, but strangely the ferocious winds had blown dazed birds onto the *Grand Rapina*, which the refugees quickly seized. Lone among the seagulls, albatrosses, and petrels was an injured pygmy owl, whisked far from his Amazon home in the storm. The little creature was panting in distress when Emmie rescued it. I disapproved of the new pet, but could not bring myself to give it back to be eaten.

Snatches of rumors continued to circulate. Although the runaways were still confined on the *Grand Rapina*, after hearing that Captain Balodis was in prison in his suite, the refugees understandably felt more free. Driven by hunger, they exerted their new sense of freedom by creating small fires on the Starlight Deck on which to cook. Since the cruise ship was still not fully restored from the damage done by the gale, no fire containment systems came on to signal that the ship was ablaze, and no life boats were automatically lowered. The space became a functioning camp, no longer a communal cell.

Thus, the refugees made themselves more comfortable than they'd been in weeks. They made meager exchanges of food and clothes. They shared with one another the stories of why they'd left their home countries to run away on the *Grand Rapina*. They made common cause. As fuel for their fires, the runaways burned whatever was handy and portable, like chairs and tables. I myself pitched in. The refugees killed, plucked, and cooked the seagulls that had fallen onto the ship, roasting them on the fires, and an almost festive air emanated from the tomb that was the Starlight Deck. The people worked together, helping one another, and a new sense of community seemed to be forming.

Emmie, though, hid her little owl in a wicker cage brought aboard earlier by one of the other refugees. She fed the bird pieces of raw albatross, for the owl was naturally a predator, and after its ordeal in the gale, it probably would've eaten anything, not excluding her fingers. I saw that Candace had joined in the gaiety and was busy turning a makeshift spit over a metal drum. If she'd had her ingredients from her own kitchen, she would've made biscuits, too.

But the runaways' joy on the Starlight Deck was short-lived. They had not escaped the fowler's snare that was the *Grand Rapina*. Above them on the topmost deck, the crew was about to go berserk, with consequences that would trickle down. In my wanderings back and forth, in my own way keeping watch, I was shocked at how rabid the crew was becoming.

From his opulent quarters near the bridge, crew members led Captain Moze Balodis in handcuffs and pajama top to the main deck. They'd not even allowed him the dignity of his pants, much less his officer's uniform. He'd been dragged unceremoniously from the comfort of the Grand Cabin with its bird's eye maple panels, and there was no air of a commodore about him. Moze looked exhausted, not from standing for hours in the wheel house to dutifully guide the *Grand Rapina* through a deluge, but from the shame of his nakedness and the loss to his pride wrought by failing in his responsibilities. Moze had nothing to say, when a wise word might have saved his life.

At the sight of their Captain thus detained, the whole crew gathered round.

"What should we do with this fool?" a bloodthirsty waiter yelled. He grabbed Moze by his hair so hard that the Captain's neck jerked back. "Used to be, some people would've made this scum walk the plank! We did everything for him, and look where we are! Who wants to hear the cry of a drowning rat?"

"He nearly killed us in the storm!" the crew screamed. "We don't have any place that will take us!" "We need fresh water!" "Punish him!" "Poke his eyes out!"

Moze did not beg for mercy. He was bent, but not cowering.

I watched in terrible anticipation.

"He's got all those prisoners locked up downstairs. I say we let them have him!"

"No, let's hang him, run him up the pole like a flag!"

The waiter's face brightened cruelly at that suggestion. He buried his hand deeper into Moze's dark hair, yanking and grinning. "Would you like to go for a swing?" he said into the Captain's upturned face.

What arose in me, then, I am sure I will never feel again. It was not love for Moze specifically that I felt, but regard for a fellow living, breathing creature. It was a rejection of abuse, mixed with a desire to wait for real justice, not mob justice. I regret to say that I found I could not, as a man of faith, love the Captain. For an instant, I dipped down into the well waters of my soul and came up empty, dry, with no cup of refreshing affection for the man who had steered the wicked *Grand Rapina*.

Whether or not these can be considered finer, higher feelings, or just my shortcomings, I don't know. But I walked toward Moze with a deck blanket and covered him. "That's enough! He can't hurt you anymore," I said to the venomous waiter, and really to all of the crowd. "Take him back to his rooms. Let him go."

"You don't get to make the decisions!" "We're running things now!" "Shut up, old man, get out of the way!" the crowd jeered.

"I said, take him back to his quarters! Take him back to his rooms or you'll have to answer to God!"

For a full minute, the hardest minute of my life, I looked at the angry crew, my eyes slowly glancing over the faces of a seething mob. They glared back at me with hatred, ready to pounce, and I feared that I, myself, might be hoisted up the rigging like a signal flag to swing in the breeze. My breath was shallow. It caught in my chest as if tethered to an anchor. I waited.

"Get him out of here," the waiter said at last, pushing the handcuffed Captain off to the side. Moze was visibly trembling now with fear and trauma, which were not alleviated by the striped blanket that I'd placed over his shame. His face was as white as the stripes on the navy-blue fabric. Once again, the Captain was taken away without a sound moaned or a tear shed. Inside, he held it all in.

I stepped back to the outskirts of the crowd.

The waiter walked past me, bitterly staring, confrontational, as if I had better watch myself from now on. I took no joy in having thwarted his attempt to lead a lynching. In fact, I was feeling a lot of fear myself.

While the crew continued to grumble, my attention was diverted by a distant, high-pitched, unfamiliar noise. It floated above the muttering crew, noticeable for its constant monotone inside the rise and fall of agitated voices. It was a mechanical sound, a motor of some kind.

A wounded, burning cruise ship attracts problems like a magnet, drawing trouble on the ocean to it. Somebody had been watching us for a while, detecting our vulnerability, lying in wait in the tradition of the colonial privateers, as was so often the case for centuries off the coast of Peru, where we eventually drifted close to Paita Port. Now the *Grand Rapina* was in danger of sinking to the bottom of the waters while under attack, as had been the fate of so many of the galleons of old.

Southward, modern-day pirates saw smoke streaming from the *Grand Rapina* from many miles away and, hoping for easy pickings, zeroed in on her with their radar. To the robbers, the *Grand Rapina* was a floating treasure trove. She could not have been more attractive if she had been loaded with rubies and bound for the royal courts of Spain. It was open season, as the pirates thought that the cruise ship was ripe to be taken.

After the gale, no officer had thought to set a serious pirate watch. There were no lookouts in the crow's nest on the main mast. Hence I, a retired pastor, was the first to see in the distance the pirates coming at us at a breakneck pace. Without binoculars, to me they were a small speck on the horizon that quickly took the shape of a flat-bottomed, open-air watercraft. This motorized skiff skimmed the waves, energetically bouncing and jostling, and as the outlaws drew closer, I heard their raucous taunts and saw them maniacally waving their guns. Later, I learned these were AK-47's and Kalashnikov rifles.

There appeared to be seven scruffy, bare-chested men onboard, their shirts unbuttoned and blowing about their arms. It seemed a small number to mount an invasion of a much-larger vessel, but I am chilled now to know that only a few well-placed projectiles from even one of their guns might have sunk us. Bringing an army of pirates was not necessary to their success.

With foam flying off of their boat, and in a sea still churning from the gale, the pirates sped toward the cruise ship with laughter and brazen confidence, as if the blood of experienced thieves pulsed in their veins. One even puffed on his pipe in cavalier defiance. Though their craft was small, I had no doubt that the pirates intended to terrorize the *Grand Rapina,* and to violently board us in short order by clambering up the side of our ship with grappling hooks. We would be lucky if they only robbed and ran away. If they decided to hold us for ransom, I feared that many passengers would die — murdered a few at a time as incentive — for Masterson would never acknowledge our existence because of the illegal refugee blood that we carried, much less pay for our release.

The invaders drew close to the cruise ship's hull, banging alongside so hard I hoped that they might be providentially thrown from their skiff. Some pirates came dressed all in black, with black masks to cover their faces, and black gloves. Some came with their faces boldly uncovered, unshaven, barefoot, in tattered, flowery tee shirts and water-soaked gym shorts, not caring if they could be identified by anyone they molested. I feared the latter the most, for I instinctively deduced that they would surely never let me live if I could remember and call out their faces.

Bobbing around, the pirates yelled threats at the top of their lungs, and pointed rocket-propelled grenades that would tear a hole in our hull in seconds. I had worried so for this hull during the gale, and now it looked as though it would be lost at the hands of crazed looters. As the pirate smoking his pipe kept his gun fixed just above the waterline on the *Grand Rapina,* his comrades prepared to climb. To them, it seemed all in a day's work, the way that they made their living, but I have never felt so helpless.

I ducked for cover at the first sound of machine gun fire. The ragtag crew from the *Grand Rapina* rushed to defend themselves, and the *rat ta tat tat* of bullets filled my ears. I was almost caught in the crossfire, but wriggled to safety. I am not sure of everything that happened next, but the pirates were not so brave at the sight of returned fire. After a few of them were dropped with bullets from the cruise ship crew, the skiff tried to speed away. As I dared to glance from the corner where I sheltered, I saw two of the pirates raise their arms in surrender and throw their rifles over the side of their skiff. The *Grand Rapina*'s crew shot them, anyway, whereupon the wounded pirates fell into the choppy, green-tinted sea, and were left behind by their surviving compatriots.

I could not comprehend the sight.

But when the gun was thrown into my hands, I'd seen what to do.

"Shoot!" a bus boy was yelling at me. "Do you want to live? Take aim and shoot!"

And I did. And I opened his back as a pirate drove the skiff away.

His sunburned body jerked sharply when he fell, as if he'd been fatally startled, and he dropped over the outboard engine's tiller steer.

His friend took the tiller and twisted it wildly, making the skiff accelerate out into the open ocean. And they ran, ran, ran.

And God, the Lord of the Universe, saw.

My hands had taken a life.

Down on the Starlight Deck, the refugees were not sitting idle. Reacting to the pirates' encroachment, they had decided to end their voyage of enslavement, once and for all. Working together in a frenzy of determination, they put the *Grand Rapina* to the torch, vigorously stoking the small, camp-like fires that had cooked their birds. Wielding a flaming table leg here and a burning seagull there, the runaways walked the deck that was their jail, taking the terrifying chance of burning the very place that they stood upon. There was no going back. The *Grand Rapina* was no longer able to hold them.

Everything on the Starlight Deck went up in flames, every floorboard, every wall, anything that could be set alight was burned. The runaways gambled that help for them would come when the conflagration was spotted by the whole Earth, not just by pirates. If not, we would all perish together. It was time to end their misery, the refugees believed, the moment of liberation had come. When the Starlight Deck began to give way, the refugees overflowed to find me on the topmost level, and I ran to them in the ashy smoke. We held one another, watched the towering blaze, and bellowed with the intensity of those who know they can die at any moment.

Candace and Emmie emerged out of the cloudy haze. My wife ran into my arms, weeping aloud. "Kiss me while there's still time," she whispered. "I thought that you might be gone."

Emmie clung to me with one arm, sobbing, and cradled her owl cage with the other.

And suddenly, the voyage of the *Grand Rapina* was over. The cruise ship smoked and glowed with fire, but she did not sail. Her splendor and power were destroyed. She was dead in the water and nothing but a ruin. I silently prayed that we would be rescued before the ocean swallowed the *Grand Rapina* whole. *Please, not like this, Lord. Please, save us from a death like this.*

The mutinous crew members went into hiding, watching the cruise ship they'd just defended burn. The officers, knowing that they had no Captain, scattered. No one approached us, not one. A few jumped overboard, afraid of the flames. As for the refugees, as well as Candy, Emmie, and me, we were not harmed by the crew or staff. We were simply abandoned by them, left in the presence of God.

* * *

"We found her in Officer Vera's room. On his bed. On top of a night gown." The elevator technician turned his eyes away to avoid Dr. Elihu's. Too much would be said in a direct gaze. He didn't want to be the one to break it to her that Hazel was having an affair with her rumored paramour, the ship's second-in-command. The tech thought those were pretty lofty heights for a lowly room steward like the big woman, unless, well, Anthony Vera was only a man, and he'd been at sea a long time. Things happen. The tech thought that Officer Vera's high-ranking bedroom was a place more suitable for the likes of Dr. Elihu. It was the way of the world, the rightness of balance.

The physician smiled to herself. How kind of the tech to try to spare her feelings, as if Tony would ever stray, and with this specimen lying before her. Dr. Elihu snapped on a pair of rubber gloves and flipped back the bedsheet from Hazel's fat face. She checked the eyes for dilation. She checked for a pulse.

"Oh, she's dead all right. I pulled a curtain pole out of her, just to get her on the gurney," the tech noted.

The other worker piped up. He was a long-time barista. "She can't be alive, can she, Doc? There was blood everywhere, all over his clothes and luggage."

Jenny Elihu's ears tingled. "What luggage?"

The elevator tech lowered his voice, like his eyes. "It was Officer Vera's suitcase."

"And it was a real mess," the barista confirmed. "I almost puked."

The three looked down at the body and understood why. It was raggedly perforated.

"We thought they might be planning something for shore, you know, together." The tech's voice trailed off, as if he were too proper to utter the crude and the impossible, something against the laws of nature.

Dr. Jenny Elihu bit her tongue and turned her head like a curious cat. She paused in growing awareness while her world view changed. The floor under her feet was not so solid as before, and not because of the storm. *The snake. The cheat. Tony was going to run out on me with the helicopter, leave me to take the fall.* "This one's not going anywhere," Jenny said curtly. "Stick her in the fridge." She tossed the sheet back over the dead woman's face.

The elevator tech did as he was told with the corpse and came back to adore the beautiful doctor again. He rarely got this close to her, and he'd had feelings that he'd long kept to himself. He blushed. "Is there anything else I can do for you, ma'am?" he asked politely.

Dr. Elihu turned to the barista. "Nathan, that's all. Thanks for bringing her down to the morgue."

"No problem! No telling what else we're going to find. That cyclone tore everything up!" The barista left. He was on the prowl to steal now, never to make iced coffee again.

Dr. Elihu returned her attention to his co-worker, the tech. She cast a net. "Jorge, there is something you can do to help me. It's . . . personal."

"Yes, Doctor, anything at all."

"Find First Officer Vera and bring him to me. I think he needs a spa treatment."

The worker's eyes widened with the shock of understanding. The hair on the back of his neck stood up. "Yes. Yes, I will give him the treatment," he replied.

Jorge said nothing more, because the gunfire above decks drowned him out. He kept to his task, however. He found the First Officer lurking not very far away, in fact, as if he had been trying to make his way to Dr. Elihu as the pirates invaded.

Nevertheless, in an hour's time, Officer Tony Vera lay bound and gagged at the bottom of the pool that had terrorized the refugees.

Unperturbed by his whimpering, Jorge threw the canvas pool cover over the officer to ensure his suffocation, and walked away, very hopeful, pirates or not.

The elevator tech burned with passion.

The doctor burned with rage.

The *Grand Rapina* burned in retribution.

CHAPTER ELEVEN

The Peruvian Coast Guard could not believe what they found and radioed for help to put out the black fires billowing from the *Grand Rapina*. As the Coast Guard sprayed the charred ship with enormous fire hoses, some refugees fled via the emergency slides off the side of the vessel, directly into rescue rafts. Some, too weak from smoke inhalation, collapsed onto the deck and waited for help. Ferries were sent to bring us supplies and doctors. Photos of the *Grand Rapina* ablaze went around the world. When we were towed to the Port of Callao, we were already a legend.

Those runaways who were weak but still able-bodied made their way slowly off of the ship, worn and haggard, as if emerging from a different dimension in space and time, down a gangway rushed into place to receive them at the cruise terminal. The most seriously frail of the refugees were taken away on stretchers in ambulances. A few, wandering aimlessly in shock, were assisted by nurses and paramedics. Infants were given oxygen. Translators, customs officials, cameramen and TV announcers, frantic relatives, the curious, all of these and more swarmed about.

And the refugees told their story of confinement on the ship, immediately, to whomever would listen. Their terror and heartbreak spilled over. They told of being robbed of their blood. They told of their hunger. They pointed to the Starlight Deck that had been their prison, and from the safety of shore, guided the authorities to the subterranean secrets inside the *Grand Rapina*. The police wasted no time. While the ship still smoldered, they searched the vessel.

Dr. Jenny Elihu was brought from the *Grand Rapina* in the grip of two national policemen, fierce-looking in their tactical gear and heavy leather boots. How different it was now from our first encounter in Charleston, when she had not deigned to let her eyes rest on my old cleric's visage. Clutched down the gangway roughly by uniformed authorities, she swore and stared at me all the way, with an anger that would have seared a hole in me if I had not chosen to look away in disgust. This time, it was I who refused to gaze. Jenny had completely lost her stoic bearing, and she fought with the police to the point that I thought she might be tased.

Behind her came many of the treacherous technical staff, and crew members whom I recalled for their viciousness, those who had done Jenny's worst bidding. These were also arrested on the spot. They had put up a brief fight with the guns that had littered the vessel, but the Peruvian Coast Guard had weapons of their own for disarming criminals on ships: tear gas cannisters. Many crew and staff came rubbing their eyes, coughing, and wiping their faces, still overcome by fumes.

The officers were frog-marched off of the *Grand Rapina* one by one. Their polished arrogance had been replaced with disheveled subjection to the law, and the full force of reality nipped at their heels at every step. Representing the basest qualities across almost every nation, and a disgrace to honorable maritime service everywhere, they hung their head in shame. How long would their remorse last? I cannot say that they had a new respect for human life, particularly for refugee life. It is my hope that they did, but who can say?

The most senior leader of them all never made it to the port. Not alive. In the end, in a way, Captain Moze Balodis went down with his ship by shooting himself in his quarters. In Moze's home country, if a Captain loses his vessel but survives, he is executed. Moze had graciously saved them the trouble. The Peruvian Coast Guard found him attired in his full officer regalia, an occasion that some miscreant secretly filmed on his phone and posted online for the world to see. I watched a cameraman standing near me playing back the footage, transfixed.

Then, specialists clad in HAZMAT suits carried the blood off of the *Grand Rapina.* Something so sacred as a population's lifeblood was seen as dangerous garbage, when a religious ceremony to acknowledge what was being removed would have been more fitting. No matter where the refugees turned, either trying to escape from their lot in their homelands by sea or coming back to terra firma still in dire distress, their lifeblood always seemed to be taken from them and desecrated. How would the survivors ever begin again? How would they make peace with their dead, hastily stacked into cardboard coffins, which followed behind the blood vials in a ghastly parade? How would they ever commemorate those family members horrifically tossed overboard by the callous staff and crew?

Finally, as Candace, Emmie, and I departed the *Grand Rapina* into the cruise terminal, I felt the child let go of my hand. She dropped the caged owl that had been her pet and companion. "Yaya! Yaya!" Emmie screamed. Throwing her arms into the air, she ran toward an old woman wrapped in a shawl.

The woman's face rejoiced as if hearing the song of a faraway angel, but when she turned her gaze to the little girl, I could see but the old woman could not: Cataracts made the grandmother's eyes filmy with shadows. Had she wanted to come to the States for help with her vision? Though nearly blind, the old woman instantly recognized Emmie's voice, and drew her to her wrinkled bosom in incredulous joy!

Candace and I stumbled in surprise. I could feel my wife's heart dissolving as if it were being dipped into a vat of briny tears. Candy called to the child above the chaos of the crowd. "Emmie? Emmie?" In a mere moment, our dreams of having a daughter, probably unrealistic hopes for adoption, were dashed in the happiness of one extraordinary little girl's reunion with her family.

Emmanuella continued walking in elation with her grandmama, carefully leading her back onto land. Their bond of love was jubilantly renewed.

Emmie never looked back.

In truth, she owed us nothing. My wife and I had given our love, but Emmie had never asked for it. Only the most severe of circumstances had even brought we three together. It was natural for the little girl to want to forget all of those traumas as soon as she could. Of course she would want to go back to her real family. The pity is, what my wife and I had felt and yearned for was natural, too.

"Candy, my dear, dear, sweetheart," was what I could utter as my own soul ached. "It's for the best . . . ."

"I know. But why not us?"

I walked to the pier and released the captive owl. He tumbled into the air, his brown and golden feathers rustling, his wings widening, and he also left us without looking back, quickly soaring above the sea lions watching him from the waters of nearby San Lorenzo Island. Unlike Candace and I, the owl was not so far from home. I remembered my wife's haunting dream of owls, and how it had prompted her to write out her last will and testament. Fighting my own doubts at the time, I had reassured Candace that we would survive the atrocity that was the *Grand Rapina*, and it looked as though we had.

But I heard footfalls behind me.

"Reverend Atterley, would you and your wife please join us in our car?"

I considered whether to obey for only a moment. A weight that I had been expecting for so long lowered squarely onto my shoulders. It was time. It could not be avoided. Candace felt it, too. "Of course. I knew this day would come," I said to the investigator showing his badge.

We drove for a short time in the van, maybe for twenty minutes. Distracted by frightening thoughts, wondering if I had just traded one form of captivity for another, I barely saw the urban landscape pass by. Candace clung to my elbow, silent.

Now, I sit in the police station in Callao, Peru. My wife has been taken to a separate room. The station is a dismal white-plaster building with curling wrought iron bars on the shutterless windows. A stray dog lies just outside the station's door, lolling in the sun beating down on the concrete plaza. I am filthy, covered in sweat, soot, and bits of seagull feathers. I have been given food and water brought by the ferries sent to the *Grand Rapina* when her fires were put out, but I've not cleaned up in days, and I am fighting the urge to run. A fan overhead is spinning with a thump that I find upsetting. Is this to be an interrogation? Will Candace be next? Do I need a lawyer?

The detective looks at me. He is a man of average height, with dark hair and brown, deep-set eyes. His skin is swarthy. He is serious. He offers me a cup of coffee. I think that I recognize the bean's Guatemalan growing region.

"We're not going to arrest you. We want to ask for your help." The detective lets his words sink in. "Did you understand me, Pastor?"

"I'm an American citizen, but my passport's long gone."

"We believe you."

"I work for Majestic Waves Cruise Lines, but I wasn't aware of anything they planned to do. I was deceived. That's the truth."

The detective lays his hand on my forearm, to calm me. "Don't worry. We're not accusing you of anything. Some of the prisoners told us how you protected them. They think of you as their hero. They say you saved them."

My shoulders flinch. I fear that he might be baiting me. Not accused of anything? I expected to go on trial. I have thought that I might go to jail for the rest of my life for being part of a maritime atrocity, and I've agonized in worry over it for months. But they know that I'm innocent? Am I? I've been so afraid of being judged by people who don't understand. I've been left to judge myself.

"Let's talk for a while before we charter a flight for you back to Charleston. Are you feeling up to this? You just got off the ship. Should we call a physician to sit with you?"

"No, I've had enough of doctors I don't know, believe me. I'm able to give you my statement."

The policemen spread photos out on a table. They stand over me to watch my reactions. I see Dr. Elihu, Captain Balodis, First Officer Vera, Chef Danilo, Chris Adamos, and I say as much to the police. Then, they lay before me pictures of men that I do not recognize. These are the pirates, they say. My heart races. "This one," I nod in pained words. "I think this one."

"We already know. Bus Boy Enrique told us."

I look up at the detective in frank and fearful expectation. I remember that God knows, but I wasn't sure about anyone else.

The investigator seems to read my mind. "People are allowed to defend themselves in Peruvian waters, Pastor Atterley." His English is very good. The thing he is implying is very clear.

"As long as I live, I will never get over it."

"In time, you will. It's the good men who grieve such things."

How often over the years have I given this same comfort to a penitent in my church office, to someone wracked with guilt? The detective has a pastoral way, and in his line of work.

"You and your wife are free to go. Just one more man to look at before you fly home."

The final photo that they show to me I also do not recognize. "I can't help with this one. I've never seen him." I learn that it is Mr. Walker Masterson.

"We suspect that he's the big fish. For the time being, he lives to do more evil. If you want to mourn over anything, mourn over that."

We all stand up. They bring my wife in. We all shake hands, expressions of sympathy are made for what Candace and I have been through on the *Grand Rapina*, and we are taken to an airport and a luxurious private jet. I don't know what to say. Who is paying for this plane? Someone who thinks I'm a hero? I try to still the newly emerging cynic in me that says this could be a bribe to stay quiet. Lord, this is who I've become. It's so hard to know the truth. Overwhelmed and tired almost to unconsciousness, Candy and I reluctantly get onboard the plane.

In six hours or so, we will land in South Carolina. My old practical self speaks up. We will have to rent a car and go to Charleston to bring home our Mazda. I won't be surprised if it's not there — the car, not Charleston. You never know. So much has been taken from us.

I remember that Candace and I have no house.

We, ourselves, are nearly as homeless as the refugees.

Perhaps there is justice in that.

Still, it is harvest season.

We will reap what we have sown.

LITERATURE HELPS US UNDERSTAND THE WORLD

QUESTIONS FOR DEEPER LEARNING

1. The title *Blood for Sail* is a play on words. Who is trying to make a profit from blood and who is buying it? Why? What makes these activities both illegal and immoral?

2. The *Grand Rapina* can be thought of as a literary symbol for a rogue ship of state or a country acting through aggression and self-interest. What are some modern examples of belligerent nations whose leaders seek to overpower others?

3. In the novel's beginning, how does Majestic Waves Cruises target Pastor James Atterley and mislead him into taking the chaplain's job on the *Grand Rapina*? Which qualities in the minister might have made him susceptible to being misled? What happens to those traits in the pastor as the story progresses?

4. The protagonist in *Blood for Sail* is a Protestant pastor and a Caucasian man trying to help people of color in Latin America. Does the author inadvertently perpetuate social inequities by sending a white Christian male into a region he knows little about as an agent of rescue? Does Pastor Atterley really rescue any characters, or do they ultimately save themselves? Why would that be an important difference?

5. Notice the wicked crew and staff onboard the *Grand Rapina* include people from all nations and all levels of status. What might the author be implying about the tendency toward evil behavior? Why might the author want to make that assertion?

6. Candace, Pastor Atterley's wife, has an odd dream about owls. These birds have been seen over the ages as symbols of both good and evil. For instance, in some parts of the Christian Church owls have been associated with spiritual wisdom. In other traditions, these birds have been viewed as harbingers of death, or even as representatives of occult activity. When Candace dreams of owls, which spiritual influence do you think she feels?

7. Similarly, the refugee child, Emmie, carries an owl in a wicker cage. What might the author intend by having the little girl carry this symbol around with her during the worst of her imprisonment onboard the *Grand Rapina*? What could it mean when Emmie reunites with her yaya (her grandmother) and immediately casts the owl aside?

8. In world literature, the sea has often represented spiritual turmoil. One potential reason is that ocean depths are largely obscured to human sight and understanding. What other reasons might that be the case? Consider how our personal inquiries about God, mortality, and individual destiny are like an unsearchable ocean of questions. How does the *Grand Rapina* float on unfathomable questions about social justice?

9. Comment on the contrast between the opulence and splendor of the *Grand Rapina* and the poverty of the poor refugees who become imprisoned there. What is indicated about social injustice when some people have so much wealth and so many resources and others have so little? Why have these issues of unfairness and imbalance never been successfully resolved by either religion or revolution? Can they ever be? Why or why not?

10. Blood imagery saturates the story of the brutal *Grand Rapina*. In literature, blood has frequently been used by authors in scenes of violence, pain, and sacrifice, but also to convey new birth, redemption, and reconciliation. What is it about human blood that can span the full range of human emotions in a story?

11. In the novel, the honorable field of medical science is misused in an attempt to make a vaccine that harms vulnerable people for the benefit of others. In society, how are we to ensure that the wisdom of the medical profession is used for purposes of healing only? Can we guarantee that medical knowledge is always used for good? Who gets to define *good*?

12. What do you think happens to James and Candace Atterley when they return to South Carolina at the end of the novel? After everything that they've been through, what might their future look like? How might they start over?

ABOUT DIANE ROSIER MILES

Diane remembers that *The Good Earth* was the first novel she ever read as a young girl, during the time when her military father was serving in Vietnam. The reading experience made Diane feel as if she had discovered an older, wiser friend in Pearl S. Buck, who seemed to have written the novel just for her.

Inspired, Diane wrote short stories for fun and school assignments, and soon, teachers noticed her talent. Diane began to win literary contests sponsored by the public schools. After completing high school in Heidelberg, Germany, where her father was stationed, Diane went to college at Austin Peay State University and earned a B.S. in English. Next, she pursued an M.S. in Technical and Science Communication at Drexel University, which she attended on a teaching assistantship. After completing her master's, Diane took more classes at the University of Pennsylvania, thinking that she might want to be a college professor.

Instead, Diane entered the corporate world, where she stayed for about 15 years in various writing and editing capacities. She got married and had a son. Eventually, Diane left full-time work to freelance and to try her hand again at creative writing. Some literary successes followed, such as a Pushcart Prize nomination. To date, Diane's work has been published by numerous literary magazines and newspapers, as well as in nationally distributed compilations including *A Cup of Comfort Devotional for Women* from Adams Media and *The Secret Place* from Judson Press. Seeking to grow as a writer, and turning down a traditional publishing offer, Diane self-published a novella entitled *Gabriel, The Training of an Angel* in 2017. This book rose to #11 in the Christian Fantasy category on Amazon. Much of Diane's work contains spiritual themes.

Diane recently founded her own publishing imprint, Dove in the Wild Wood Books LLC. In 2022, Diane self-published a full-length thriller entitled *Blood for Sail* through her new company. Readers praised the story as reminiscent of Joseph Conrad's *Heart of Darkness*, and Diane was thrilled when the novel was recommended by *Kirkus Reviews*. Diane also continues to traditionally publish, and in the future she hopes to help other writers come into print through her own small press.

Diane lives in Chester County, Pennsylvania, with her family. They love to watch the colorful and noisy birds in their yard. Diane also sporadically gardens. And she notes modestly that she is a pretty fabulous cook. Contact Diane at dianerosiermiles@gmail.com.

Made in the USA
Middletown, DE
27 November 2024

65237613R00096